AUDRA

MAIL-ORDER BRIDES OF SAPPHIRE SPRINGS

MARGERY SCOTT

CLOVER RIDGE PRESS

HISTORICAL ROMANCES

MORGANS OF ROCKY RIDGE

*Travel to Rocky Ridge, Colorado and meet the Morgan men
and the women who love them.*

Cade
Trey
Zane
Will
Jesse
Brett
Heath

ROCKY RIDGE ROMANCE

It isn't only the Morgan men who fall in love in Rocky Ridge.

Landry's Back in Town
Substitute Bride
Wanted: The Perfect Husband
Hannah's Hero
High Stakes Bride
Jasper's Runaway Bride
Mail-Order Melanie

MAIL-ORDER BRIDES OF SAPPHIRE SPRINGS

Miranda
Audra
Kathryn
Elise
Laura
Cassie

BRIDES OF COLDWATER CREEK

Josie
Sally
Anna
Beth
Willa

OTHER HISTORICAL ROMANCES

Emma's Wish
Wild Wyoming Wind
Rose: Bride of Colorado

MEDICAL ROMANCES

The Surgeon's Homecoming
Stranded with the Surgeon
The Firefighter and the Lady Doc

ROMANTIC SUSPENSE

A Time for Secrets
No One to Tell
The Stranger She Knows
A Question of Guilt
A Stranger in Paradise

CHAPTER 1

Sapphire Springs, Texas

Neall Gardiner sat astride Apollo, his coal-black stallion, and surveyed the valley.

His valley.

The land was his, from the river that wound its way through the land a few hundred acres behind him to the emerald green grassland that rose into the foothills at the base of the Blue Mountains in the distance.

He smiled. He'd done well, and he was proud of what he'd accomplished in the past six years since his father died. He'd gambled, risked more money than he should have when he'd bought the steers from Abe Littlejohn to start his herd, but it had paid off.

Now, he had a reputation for raising some of the highest quality beef in the state.

He'd bought up the last thousand acres just the year before, and he'd be adding another two thousand or so next month when Abe sold out to him and went to live with his daughter in Austin.

He had the perfect life. Well, almost perfect. That empty, gnawing part of him begged for something more. Something he'd had growing up, but had lost, little by little, ever since his father died. A family.

He'd always figured he'd be married by now, but he'd been so busy with the ranch that time had slipped by without him really even noticing. Now, with his thirtieth birthday approaching, it was past time to find himself a bride.

There were unmarried women in Sapphire Springs. Plenty of them, as a matter of fact, and more than a few who'd be willing to marry him. But how could he know which ones cared about him and which ones were only interested in the financial security and luxury he could offer? After what had happened to his cousin up in Fort Worth—the woman who'd supposedly loved him, had spent every cent he'd had and more, and then ran off with a banker from somewhere in California—Neall was afraid to take the chance the same thing would happen to him. If he lost his ranch because of a woman…

There was one way to be sure the woman he married wanted him and not his money, he thought, turning Apollo in the direction of the ranch house. He flicked the reins, and the stallion set off at a trot across the field. He could marry a woman who didn't know him, a woman who'd know nothing about him other than what he told her.

He could get himself a mail-order bride.

It had worked for John Weaver, Neall reasoned. After John's wife died, he'd been left with a diner to run and two little girls to raise with nobody to help him except his aunt. John had sent away for a mail-order bride. He'd married Miranda the day she arrived. They'd had their own issues to deal with, but they'd worked it out and he was a happy man now.

Maybe Neall would be just as lucky. It was a gamble, but he'd never been afraid to take a risk when the reward was worth it.

As he rode closer, the ranch house came into view, large and impressive. He could see his whole family history in the construction of it—the original two-story house his great-grandfather had built when he and his great-grandmother had arrived in Texas from the Scottish lowlands with a dream and a few dollars to buy a parcel of land, the rooms added on when his grandparents had married, the addition his father had built when Neall was a baby.

Neall lived alone in that house now, except for Mrs. Davey, the housekeeper who'd looked after him since he was a boy. They might not be related by blood, but she was the only family he had left.

Apollo stopped at the bottom of the steps leading to the front porch. As Neall dismounted, his foreman, Tucker Gates, opened the front door.

"Afternoon, boss," Tucker said, coming down the stairs and approaching Neall. "I'll take Apollo to the barn and rub him down. I'm heading that way anyway."

"Thanks, Tucker."

Tucker took the horse's reins from Neall. "Left some bills on your desk for you to look over," he said.

"I'll do that," Neall replied.

Tucker ran his hand down Apollo's neck and took a few steps toward the barn before Neall called out to him. "I'm going into town later. Are you expecting any deliveries or need anything at the mercantile?"

"I can send one of the boys—"

"No need," Neall insisted. He'd never been a man to expect anyone else to do something he wouldn't do himself, and if he was being completely honest, he enjoyed working alongside his men, getting his hands dirty, feeling his muscles burn from a hard day's work.

"Got an order at the mercantile if you feel like taking the wagon," Tucker said.

"I'll do that."

Tucker nodded, then continued on his way with Apollo.

Neall climbed the stairs and went into the house, the smell of wood polish filling his nose. Mrs. Davey appeared in the doorway of the small room he used as an office. He'd always loved that room because of the huge windows giving him a view of the river and the cattle grazing in the fields. It used to be a receiving parlor, but he'd taken it over after his mother passed on two years before.

"I'm just finishing cleaning," she said, the faint

Scottish burr she'd never been able to lose creeping into her voice. "'Course it would be a lot easier if you'd keep it tidy."

"Yes, ma'am, I will," he replied with a smile. His messiness had been a bone of contention between them since he was a boy. He'd never outgrown it, and she'd finally given up trying to change his ways. Now, it was a shared joke between them. She complained; he agreed to do better.

"I've made a decision," he told her, changing the subject.

"Oh?"

"Yes, and since it'll affect you, too, I want you to hear it first."

A worried frown appeared between her brows. She twisted the dust rag between her hands until Neall grinned. "I'm getting married."

Mrs. Davey's brows shot up. "What?"

"Yes," he repeated. "It's time, don't you think?"

"Well past time if you ask me," she responded, a broad smile sweeping across her face. "Might I ask who the lucky woman is?"

His grin widened. "Well…I'm not sure yet, but as soon as I find out, you'll be the first to know."

"I'm so sorry, Audra."

Audra Holt dragged her eyes away from her friend's guilt-ridden face and lowered her gaze to the sleeping infant cradled in her arms. Luckily, Thomas was only four months old and wasn't old enough to realize that soon they would be homeless and penniless. "I understand," she said. "With your own new baby coming, you won't have room for us."

She did understand. The house was already bursting at the seams with three adults and four children tripping over each other in two bedrooms, a cramped living area and a kitchen only one person could use at a time.

"I tried to persuade Otto to let you stay," Birdie said, referring to her husband, "but he thinks it'll be too crowded. I feel terrible…"

Audra looked up through tears that burned her eyes. She squeezed Birdie's hand. Birdie, the name she'd always called her best friend, Beatrice, was close to tears herself. "I've been planning to find another place for Thomas and me anyway and I didn't have the heart to tell you, so don't give it another thought," she lied.

Birdie's eyes widened. "You were? Where? And what will you do for work? You don't know how to read."

The reminder that she couldn't read, or write more than her name, made Audra's stomach clench. Words and numbers on paper were nothing more than squiggled lines to her, and although she'd tried to learn when she was a girl, her teacher had grown so frustrated she'd given up on her. Her parents had taken her out of school when the teacher had told them she was dimwitted and would never amount to anything.

Even Birdie had tried to teach her, but had failed. Birdie had tried to convince her that it wasn't because Audra couldn't learn, but that Birdie didn't have the skills to know how to teach her. Audra was sure her best friend was just trying to be kind.

Audra's parents had believed the teacher, telling her regularly that she'd better be a good cook and be able to look after a house because she'd never be able to get a husband with her looks or her brain.

She'd found a husband, though. Tom was a fair bit older than she was, and she'd often wondered if he was more interested in her housekeeping skills than anything else, but he'd told her he loved her and she'd wanted to believe him. She'd grown to love him, and she'd had a home and a family. She'd been content.

Those days were gone, and now she had to look to the future. Where would she ever find employment, even if she could find someone to care for Thomas while she worked? She still had a few dollars from the sale of the farm she'd shared with Tom until…

A lump formed in her throat and a single tear escaped. She brushed it away before Birdie noticed it. No, she would not think about that. She had to focus on the future, not the past. She pasted a smile on her face. "It'll be fine," she said as brightly as she could manage. "Now, let me put Thomas down for a nap and I'll help you prepare supper."

A few minutes later, Audra came back into the kitchen. "What are you doing?" she asked.

Birdie was sitting at the table, a bowl of string beans at her side, a copy of *The Philadelphia Record* open in front of her. She pointed to one of the pages, the bean in her hand flapping.

"What is it?" Audra asked.

"Listen to this," Birdie said. "Twenty-nine-year-old farmer, healthy, average height, weight and appearance—"

"Who are you talking about?"

"The farmer. It's an advertisement from a farmer in Texas."

"And?"

"Listen to the rest." Birdie turned her attention back to the newspaper. "Here it is…searching for a bride 20-30 years old, a hard worker. Don't have much to offer, but want to share what I do have with the right woman. If interested, please contact Miranda Weaver, Sapphire Springs, Texas."

"I still don't see—"

Birdie's voice rose with excitement. "It's the perfect solution to your problem. You could become a mail-order bride."

"A…a what…?" Audra sputtered.

"A mail-order bride," Birdie repeated. "More and more women are doing it these days."

"They are?"

Birdie nodded. "Otto was telling me a few weeks ago that two of the women who work in the factory with him signed up with an agency who arranges marriages."

"I can't imagine—"

"A matchmaker arranges for a man and a woman to correspond for a while," Birdie went on, "and if they both agree, the woman travels to where the man lives and they get married and live happily ever after."

"But why would a woman marry a stranger? Traveling all that way alone…and marrying a stranger seems very risky and possibly dangerous."

"I suppose it could be, but there are a hundred reasons why a woman might choose to do that. She might need financial security or she might be at an age to have children and have no prospects at home. She might need to escape from a bad situation she's in…"

Birdie rested her hand on her stomach as she struggled to get to her feet. Once upright, she wrapped her hands around Audra's. "You know I would never allow Otto to cast you out into the street, but—"

"That's not necessary. I won't come between you and Otto. I'll be gone as soon as possible. I appreciate everything you've done for me and Thomas these past few weeks," Audra said.

"Just think about it," Birdie prodded. "It could be the answer for you."

Audra tugged her hands out of Birdie's grip. "I will," she said, although she had no intention of even considering such a thing. She'd think of something.

She had to. "Now let me check and see if Thomas is asleep yet and I'll start peeling the potatoes."

As she gazed down at Thomas in the crib in the small bedroom she shared with him and three of Birdie's children, she couldn't help thinking about where they'd go, what they'd do. What kind of future could she give her child?

Maybe she could be a governess, or a cook or a housemaid. Her cakes and pies were the talk of Lincolnville, and if nothing else, she could clean a house.

Still, there was only one house in the entire village that had a housekeeper, so her chances of finding work were highly unlikely.

To go to Philadelphia or one of the larger towns nearby would use up what little money she had, leaving nothing to support herself and Thomas until she found work and a place to live.

She'd seen the painted ladies hanging over the upstairs balcony at the tavern a block away, offering themselves to the men who passed by. What if that was the only option she had? Her stomach roiled at the thought.

She was still mulling over her predicament when she crawled into bed that night. But could she marry a man she didn't know?

～

It took less than a week for Audra to realize she really had no choice but to marry a stranger. Every morning, Audra had left Thomas with Birdie while she searched for work.

Every evening, she came home, still unemployed…well, if she didn't count being offered a job at the Black Bear Pub. She hadn't even gone inside to ask for work. The owner, Horace Adams, had happened to be outside leaning against a post while he puffed on a cigar. He'd raked his eyes over her as she walked past, making her squirm in her skin.

"Hey, darlin'," he'd called out. "You looking for work? With that body of yours, I've got a lot of customers who'd be happy to pay you well."

She'd ignored him and hurried away, her heart heavy. What was to become of her and Thomas if she couldn't find work?

She was running out of time, and she couldn't impose on Birdie and Otto much longer. Birdie's child was due within a few weeks.

By the time she reached the small cabin, she'd made the decision. Becoming a mail-order bride was the lesser of two evils, but she needed Birdie's help.

Later that night, Audra and Birdie sat in front of the fire, the crackling of the wood the only sound in the room. Otto was out at a meeting and the children were asleep. Birdie was darning one of Otto's shirts, and Audra was unraveling a knitted shawl so she could reuse the yarn.

"Birdie," Audra said quietly, "I've decided to become a mail-order bride."

Birdie stopped stitching and lowered the shirt to her lap. "Are you sure? What made you change your mind?"

Audra felt the blood rush to her cheeks as she told her friend about her encounter with the saloon owner. "I fear I'll soon have no other choice but to accept his offer."

"That's a big step."

"It is," she agreed, "but surely it can't be worse than the alternative. I have to hope that whoever I marry will be a good man who'll accept Thomas as his own and give us both a good life. But I need your help. Will you write the letter for me?"

"Of course." Birdie put her sewing on the small table beside her chair and got up, then crossed to a rolltop desk and took out paper and ink. "Is there anything special you'd like me to say?"

Audra shook her head. "I'm sure whatever you write will be perfect, but please don't tell him you wrote the letter because I'm too stupid to learn to read or write—"

"Stop that!" Birdie grabbed Audra's hand and squeezed it affectionately. "You are not stupid! Just because that teacher was too incompetent to teach you to read and write—"

"Please don't tell him."

Birdie sighed. "All right," she said. "I won't, but

you'll have to tell him eventually. You can't marry the man and live with him without him finding out."

"I know. I will, but not yet."

Birdie dipped her pen into the ink and began to write. A few minutes later, she blew on the paper to dry the ink and set the pen on the table. "There," she said. "Done. I'll get an envelope and a stamp and we can take it to the post office tomorrow."

Tomorrow, Audra repeated to herself. Tomorrow could be the beginning of a wonderful new life. Or a nightmare.

CHAPTER 2

Neall had never had stomach trouble before, but riding into Sapphire Springs that morning, he'd felt as if a herd of buffalo was stampeding in his gut.

Stupid, he chided himself. He was a grown man, a successful rancher. Why was he so nervous about the letters he knew were waiting for him at Millie's Diner?

It had been more than two weeks since Miranda Weaver had agreed to help him find a bride.

Miranda had come to Sapphire Springs as a mail-order bride, and even though she and John had hit a few rough patches, they'd fallen in love and were a happy family now.

She'd been reluctant, but he'd persuaded her to help him write an advertisement and she'd agreed to place the ads in the newspapers back East on his behalf.

That morning, one of the ranch hands who'd

been in town had brought a message from her that there were several letters waiting for him.

He reined in Apollo in front of the diner and dismounted, then looped the reins around the hitching post.

Taking in a deep breath, he opened the door. The bell jingled.

Miranda was cleaning a table when he walked in. She looked up and smiled. "Neall! It's good to see you," she said, scooping up some crumbs into a cloth. "I was hoping you'd come by soon. Let me get rid of this and wash up and I'll bring the letters out to you. Sit down. I'll just be a minute. Coffee?"

He nodded. "Thanks," he muttered, crossing the room and planting himself at a table near the window. He took off his hat and raked his fingers through his hair, then set the hat on the chair beside him.

While he waited, he gazed through the window to the street. People rushed about. Wagons rolled past. Two men Neall didn't recognize rode by, dismounting in front of the saloon. A group of ladies chatted on the boardwalk in front of the mercantile, and a few children raced down the center of the street toward the new schoolhouse at the edge of town.

"I'm so sorry to keep you waiting." Miranda's voice caught his attention. He turned to face her.

She was holding a mug in one hand and a stack of envelopes in the other. She set the mug on the table in front of him. "Looks like the ad was a success," she said, handing him the envelopes as she slid into a chair opposite him. "I hope you find a letter from a woman you like."

"If not, we can try again, can't we? Maybe in different newspapers? You know about these things—"

"I only know my own experience," she replied. "I'm not a matchmaker."

He picked up the pile of envelopes. "You should be. You're obviously good at it."

Miranda let out a chuckle. "Let's just wait and see what kind of responses you got before you make a judgment like that. I'll leave you to read them in private—"

"No," he said, feeling a trickle of panic inch up his spine. "I'd like you to stay so I can discuss them with you as I read them. If you don't mind, that is."

"Of course I don't mind." She leaned a little closer. "To be honest, I admit I'm a bit curious myself."

After fifteen minutes, he'd narrowed his choices to two. He'd almost decided that the woman who was an adventurer and risk-taker could be the perfect wife for him, but something about the other woman that he couldn't put his finger on kept drawing him back to her letter. The woman's name was Audra. Pretty name, he thought. Her words were plain, but they intrigued him. She spoke of the necessity to leave town and her desire to marry based on mutual respect and friendship. She understood Neall didn't have much but she was willing to work with him to build a better life for them both.

She was a widow, so she understood loss and grief. He wouldn't have to try to explain the emptiness he felt inside now that he was alone. She likely felt the same way.

The two letters lay side-by-side on the table, his dark brown eyes flitting from one to the other. Finally, he stabbed his finger onto Audra's letter. "Her. This is the woman I want."

Audra's fingers trembled as Birdie handed her the envelope with her name on it. Even though she wouldn't be able to read the letter inside, she did recognize her name printed on the front.

The man had a heavy hand, she thought, studying the thick strokes in his handwriting. A frisson of fear snaked up her spine as the thought flitted through her mind that his heavy hand might extend to disciplining his wife and children.

She slipped her finger beneath the flap to rip the envelope open. Inside were two pieces of paper she assumed were letters from Neall. But it wasn't the paper that made her draw in a gasp. "Oh, my," she whispered when she saw the stack of bills that were piled inside the envelope.

"What—?"

Birdie followed Audra's gaze, her eyes bulging

when they landed on the contents of the envelope. "Oh, my, indeed!"

Her heart racing, Audra plucked the money out of the envelope. As she did, something else fell out and drifted to the floor. Birdie tried to bend over, then stopped. A giggle escaped and she patted her bulging stomach. "You'll have to get that," she said.

Audra returned her smile and picked up the rectangular piece of thick blue paper. "What is it?" she asked, handing it to Birdie.

"A train ticket," Birdie replied. "To Texas."

Audra heard herself suck in a breath. Panic, the kind of panic she'd only felt once before, filled her until Birdie's voice was nothing more than a loud buzz and her head felt like liquid. She gripped the back of the chair and eased herself down.

She'd wanted this, hadn't she? That was why she'd agreed to let Birdie write to this stranger. But now, the reality of the situation was overwhelming.

"The letter," Audra murmured, taking out the folded piece of paper. She unfolded it, her gaze landing on the lines of squiggled shapes filling the page. He seemed to have a lot to say, she mused.

"Let me read the letter for you." Birdie's voice filtered through Audra's brain. In a daze, she held out the letter. Birdie plucked it from her hand and began to read.

Dear Mrs. Holt,

My condolences on the loss of your husband. I'm aware I can never take his place, but if you'll consent to be my wife, I'll do my best to make you happy and give you a good life.

As I mentioned in the advertisement, I have a small farm on the outskirts of Sapphire Springs, Texas. Although I am far from wealthy, I earn enough money to support you and a family. I have enclosed some money to pay for your travel expenses.

I'll be waiting for you at the train station in Austin on July 15th. If you don't arrive, I'll assume you've decided not to come. I do hope you will, though, because from your letter, it seems as if we could build a future together.

Sincerely,
  Neall Gardiner

Birdie folded the paper and slid it back into the envelope. "Well? What do you think?"

Audra swallowed past the dryness in her mouth. "I…don't know… It's very strange that he hasn't even mentioned Thomas, isn't it?"

"Maybe…a little…"

"You did tell him about Thomas—"

"Of course! And he's willing to marry you," Birdie said.

Audra nodded absently. She would have a home of her own, and Thomas would have a father to teach him how to be a man.

The alternative was… She couldn't bear to think about it, and even if she did swallow every ounce of self-respect she had, would she earn enough to give Thomas the life he deserved?

Her heart thundered in her chest, but she spoke surely and confidently. "I'll go to Texas and marry Mr. Gardiner."

"I'm going to miss you so much," Birdie cried out, pulling Audra into a hug as tight as was possible with her protruding stomach between them. "It's a good thing, though. And I promise, I'll write to you every week."

"And I'll try to find someone to write letters for me," Audra said, her voice cracking with emotion. She picked up the train ticket and gave it to Birdie. "When does the train leave?"

A frown marred Birdie's forehead.

"What is it?"

Birdie looked up and met Audra's eyes. "Friday. This Friday. That's only three days from now."

Three days!

She repeated the words in her head. Three days until her life changed forever.

Neall paced the station platform in Austin, sweat trickling down his back under the crisp white shirt and ribbon tie he'd put on that morning. Now it felt like a noose, tightening more by the minute. How much of his discomfort was from the heat and how much was from nervousness, he couldn't say.

He took out the gold pocket watch his mother had handed down to him after his father passed. His fingers gently grazed the engraving on the inside of the lid. *"Until the end of time, all my love, Judith."*

His throat tightened. His parents had been married for almost forty years before his father died, and his mother had always told him she'd loved him more and more every day they'd had together. Soon after, a widowed neighbor had come around, and eventually proposed. His mother had turned him down. When Neall had asked why, she'd plainly told him that no other man could ever take his father's place in her heart.

That was the kind of love Neall wanted, an enduring, fulfilling kind of love. But at the same time, he didn't think it was really possible. Not for him. That kind of love was rare, and only one in a million people were ever lucky enough to find it. So far, he hadn't been that one in a million.

Dragging his thoughts away from the past, he checked the time. The train should have pulled in an hour before.

He wished he could have convinced Miranda to wait with him at the station. Surely it would have been easier for both him and his future wife with a buffer between them. He would have a friend to keep him company, and Audra would have another woman to make her feel more comfortable.

Miranda had refused when he'd asked, though. She'd felt he and Audra should start their relationship without outside interference, and no matter how Neall had tried to cajole her into coming with him, she'd been adamant.

He gazed into the distance, and just as he began to wonder if there had been an accident or a robbery that could be causing the delay, a faint cloud of smoke mushroomed in the clear blue sky. Moments later, the train rounded a curve and let out a shrill whistle.

His nerves sharpened as the locomotive puffed into the station and came to a stop.

He took off his hat and ran his fingers through his dark brown hair, then set the hat back on his head.

Only a half dozen passengers climbed down the steps onto the platform. A couple with two excited children hurried toward the back of the train where men were unloading baggage. A cowboy carrying saddlebags over his shoulder and a saddle in his other hand gave Neall a cursory glance before passing by.

The only other passenger was a woman carrying an infant.

He turned away and marched down the platform toward the last car of the train before the caboose. He hadn't seen anyone get out of that car. Perhaps she was still on board.

He nodded a greeting to the porter, a man he'd spoken to several times before when he'd met visitors at the station, then climbed aboard. His gaze scanned the empty seats, a huff of frustration escaping him, unwilling to accept that the woman he'd been expecting wasn't there.

He frowned. Had Audra changed her mind? Missed the train? Or was she a female charlatan who'd taken his money, never intending to marry him at all?

He disembarked, pausing at the bottom of the steps while he decided what to do, when a soft voice from behind him spoke. "Mr. Gardiner?"

He turned to face the owner of the voice. He didn't recognize the woman, but she apparently knew him.

If she wasn't so pale and her cheekbones taut against her skin, she would be pretty, he mused. Her eyes were wide set and an unusual shade of blue, and a few faint freckles dotted her nose. Her hair, the color of wet walnut, was drawn back away from her face in a knot at the nape of her neck.

His gaze traveled down her length. She was thin. Too thin, in his opinion. Although the traveling suit she was wearing hugged her ample breasts, it was clearly of inferior quality and the material far too thick for the heat of a Texas summer.

He raised his eyes to her face again, and her lips drew his attention—full and sensual. And right now, her straight, even teeth were nibbling on her bottom lip.

"Are you Neall Gardiner?" she asked again.

He'd been so preoccupied with studying the woman, he'd forgotten to answer her. "I am," he said. "May I help you?"

Her eyes lowered to the infant in her arms as he squirmed in her grasp. She adjusted the baby and gave him a soft smile. "I'm Audra. Audra Holt."

Audra! How was that possible? She couldn't be Audra Holt. "Mrs. Holt?"

She nodded. "I am," she said. She held out her hand to shake his. "Please call me Audra."

He nodded an acknowledgement. "And you should call me Neall."

"It's nice to meet you." Then she moved the blanket that was wrapped around the baby so Neall could see his face.

Neall's eyes widened in alarm. "That's…a baby."

Audra gazed at the man she was going to marry. In the time since she'd received his letter, she'd imagined what he would look like, how his voice would sound. Now she knew her imagination couldn't be trusted.

Neall looked nothing like she'd expected. When he'd written that he was a farmer, she'd envisioned a man like her late husband, Tom—a man who was work-weary and had dirt under his fingernails, a man dressed in overalls and mud-covered boots, a man whose speech was simple.

Although she could see his hands were work-roughened, this man's fingernails were clean. His boots were shined and what she assumed were his Sunday church-going clothes were high quality and fit his broad shoulders perfectly.

In the advertisement, he'd said he was average. This man was anything but. He was much better looking than she'd even dreamed of, with a rugged quality that attracted her.

She was pleased, but by the frown creasing his forehead, she was the only one who was.

He was still looking at Thomas as if he were some strange creature he'd never seen before. "You have a baby," he sputtered finally.

As if the child knew they were speaking about him, he opened his eyes and gave Neall a toothless smile.

"This is Thomas," Audra said. A mother's pride filled her voice as she gazed lovingly down on the infant.

"It's a boy?"

She grinned. "Last time I looked, he was."

Neall's gaze hadn't left Thomas's face. And he wasn't smiling. "You didn't tell me you had a child."

Was it possible—? No. Birdie would never have deliberately left out the fact Audra had a child. Would she?

Audra gazed up at him. His jaw was tense. A frown marred his forehead. "What? Of course—"

"I'm sure I would have remembered if the woman I offered to marry had told me she had a child. When you answered my advertisement, you didn't say anything about a child. Did you really think you could show up here and I'd accept you and your child without question?"

Audra's face flamed at the accusation.

"You didn't think something like a child was important enough to tell me before you accepted my proposal?" Neall went on.

What could she say? That she hadn't written the letter? That he'd offered to marry a woman who couldn't read or write? The shame she'd lived with all her life wouldn't let her admit she was stupid. "I did—"

He held up his hand to stop her from speaking, then turned away from her and began to pace, his head lowered, his hands stuffed in his pockets.

Suddenly, steam billowed from beneath the front of the train and the whistle screamed. The wheels squealed and began to turn, a slow chugging sound filling the air as the train began to move out of the station.

It picked up speed, and she watched it grow smaller and smaller until it disappeared over the horizon.

Finally, Neall turned back to face Audra.

"You lied to me," he said. "Why don't you admit it?"

There was a forced calmness to his voice that was more frightening than if he'd been shouting.

"I didn't." She hadn't. Not really. Birdie had, but she couldn't bring herself to tell him that. He'd likely think she was trying to blame someone else. There was only one way she could think of to deal with what Birdie had done—take the blame herself.

She'd been told so many times growing up that no man would want a woman who couldn't read or write that when Tom had courted her and proposed, she'd jumped at the chance to have a family of her own. But this man…this man who was so well-dressed and handsome…he'd never want a woman like her.

She didn't know why Birdie hadn't mentioned Thomas, but that didn't matter right now. The damage was done, and now, for some strange reason she couldn't even explain to herself, she felt it was better to have Neall think she lied than to have him know she was stupid.

"Lies by omission are still lies," he pointed out.

His voice burst into her thoughts, and she said the only thing she could think of. "That's true, I suppose, but…" Her cheeks flushed. "I have a confession to make."

"An admission of guilt? Or something else? Might as well get all the lies out in the open at once, don't you think?"

"I...I didn't mention Thomas because I was afraid you wouldn't want me if you knew I had a child."

"You might have been right, but we'll never know now, will we?"

"I was living with my friend, Birdie, but I had to leave because she was expecting another child and there was no room for us. I couldn't find work...well, unless I worked at one of the brothels near the river..."

"So you came here hoping to prey on my sympathy?"

She shook her head, then nodded. "Not your sympathy," she contradicted. "I hoped it wouldn't make a difference to you."

"I see." He raked his fingers through his dark brown hair. "I can't say I would have offered marriage if you'd been honest at the start, but it might not have made a difference to me. Now...how can I believe anything you tell me?"

"I'm so sorry..."

"So am I. I'd hoped we could have a good life together, but I can't marry a woman I can't trust, and I can't trust you. I'd wonder if you were lying to me every time you open your mouth."

CHAPTER 3

*A*udra couldn't think. Her face flamed. Her heart sank and a knot formed in her stomach.

Neall didn't want to marry her. Yes, she understood why he'd changed his mind. He'd been lied to. If the situation were the other way around, she'd be angry, too. But understanding didn't make it any easier for her to accept the fact that she'd taken the chance and traveled hundreds of miles for nothing.

She knew no one here, had very little money, and by the looks of Sapphire Springs, there would be even less chance of finding work here than back in Lincolnville. Except for the saloon, she amended. Every town had at least one saloon, and although she couldn't see one from where she was standing, she was sure there would be some kind of drinking establishment not far away.

How could Birdie have done this? How could

Birdie have convinced her to write to Neall, filled her with hope for a bright future, and encouraged her to go all the way to Texas to marry him? And lied about something as important as a child?

Tears burned her eyes, and she reached up and wiped them away with her sleeve. "I'm so sorry," she said again.

"Goodbye, Mrs. Holt," he said. "Good luck." He turned and walked away. She watched him leave, her heart racing, panic threatening to overwhelm her.

She took a few steps in the same direction he was going, then stopped. She had nowhere to go.

She watched him march down the street, past buildings with boardwalks in front—a bank, a gunsmith's shop, a hotel. People hurried about, wagons rolled past, and men on horseback rode by. Three painted ladies lounged outside the saloon where he tipped his hat to them and then moved on.

Audra's heart plummeted. Had she traveled hundreds of miles only to end up in the same situation she'd left—where the only work she'd be able to find would be selling herself to men?

Thomas began to squirm in her arms, letting out a tiny wail. She rocked him gently and he quieted.

Suddenly, Neall stopped, drawing her attention back to him. She watched, her heart thundering in her chest. Then he slowly turned back and walked toward her. "What will you do now?"

"I don't know," she replied. "I have nowhere to go."

He studied her for quite some time. Finally, he let out a sigh and spoke. "Then you might as well come with me. You can stay at the ranch with me and Mrs. Davey until the next train going back. I'm not sure exactly, but I think it passes through in about two weeks."

"I…I can't go home…"

"If you don't have the money, I'll pay the fare."

"It's not that," she murmured. "There's…nothing to go home to." Except a life of poverty, starvation and God only knew what else. She didn't say that, though. She didn't want his pity. She'd just be thankful she had a roof over her head for now.

Audra followed Neall's gaze as he looked up at the sky. The sun sat high in the sky.

"Are you ready to leave?" he asked.

Audra nodded.

"How many trunks did you bring?" he asked.

"Just one."

"I'll get it," he said. "Let's go. I want to get back to Sapphire Springs while there's still plenty of daylight left."

He turned away and marched down the platform, leaving Audra to follow behind.

Audra's arms ached from carrying Thomas, but she gritted her teeth and followed Neall to a wagon near the train depot.

While he deposited her trunk in the wagon bed, Audra stood at the side of the wagon, her brow furrowed as she tried to come up with some way to climb into the wagon with Thomas in her arms. She certainly wasn't going to ask Neall to hold the baby while she settled herself.

If she hurried… She reached up and laid Thomas on the seat. Then, keeping one hand as close to him as possible in case he rolled off, she quickly climbed up and sat down, scooping him back into her arms.

A few seconds later, Neall took the seat beside her and they set off. Two hours later, they left Sapphire Springs behind and rode in silence down a well-worn trail, although Audra had no idea where the trail led since there was no sign of civilization anywhere.

The heat was overpowering, but thankfully, the constant movement of the wagon kept Thomas from waking.

Audra couldn't resist casting a sideways glance at Neall. Wisps of hair the color of coal brushed against the starched collar of his white shirt. She studied his profile. Grayish-blue eyes rimmed by dark lashes, a straight nose, and a well-defined jawline. All in all, he was a very handsome man.

They rode along the trail until they reached a wooden arch with a weathered sign hanging from two hooks attached to the top.

She wanted to ask him about the words on the sign, but she couldn't without giving away her secret.

They drove silently through the arch and she

gazed around, wondering why it was there in the middle of nowhere. There were no buildings, no signs of life anywhere.

Her natural curiosity got the better of her. She took a moment to plan how she'd ask her question without revealing her ignorance. "Where are we?" she asked finally.

He looked over at her. "Stonehaven Ranch. Didn't you notice the sign when we passed?"

That surprised her. She'd always heard that ranches in the West were large parcels of land. She ignored his question and instead asked another. "Who does it belong to?"

"Me."

It was possible she'd misunderstood when she'd heard about ranches. He'd said he owned a small farm. Maybe farms were called ranches in Texas. Yes, she decided, that must be it.

"Where did it get its name?" she asked, gazing around and seeing nothing but empty land. No stones anywhere.

"Stonehaven has been in my family for generations," he said, pride evident in his voice. "It was named by my great-great-grandfather after the town where he grew up in Scotland before he came to America."

A twinge of envy bubbled up inside Audra. "How wonderful it must be to have such history and roots," she said softly. "To feel as if you belong."

"I assume since you have no desire to go back East

that you don't have family and roots there," he commented a few moments later.

She shook her head. "My father was a…well, let's say he didn't like to stay in one place and when he couldn't find work, we moved on."

"I see."

They drove for what seemed like miles through trees and high shrubs. Audra couldn't help wondering if they'd ever reach the farm…ranch…whatever it was called. Unease niggled at her. After all, she was now miles from civilization with a stranger. "Do we have much farther to go?"

He shook his head. "Only another few minutes," he replied. "As soon as we get out of these trees, we'll be in a clearing and you can see the house from there."

Audra was glad to hear that. The trees were so close the lower branches scraped against the sides of the wagon, and she could only see a few patches of sky through the branches overhead.

By the time they exited the trees, Audra's heart was thumping in her chest and she was starting to find it difficult to take a deep breath. Finally, they left the trees behind and came to the clearing he'd mentioned.

Her eyes widened and she sucked in a gasp at the sight of the biggest house she'd ever seen. Why, it was even bigger than the mayor's house back in Lincolnville. She counted the windows. More than a dozen just on the front alone. She grabbed his arm. "Stop!"

"What?"

"Please…stop!"

He looked at her as if she'd grown three heads, but he drew on the reins until the horses stopped. "What's wrong?"

"Where are we?" she demanded, her voice growing shrill.

"I told you," he snapped. "We're on Stonehaven land. Where did you think we were?"

"I thought we were going to your farm."

"This is my ranch."

She scanned the lush green fields, several buildings close to the main house and another cluster of buildings in a horseshoe-shaped enclave a short distance away. "And this is all yours?"

He nodded. "Is there something about it that displeases you?"

She shifted in her seat. Luckily, Thomas had slept through her outburst. "There is something that displeases me a lot."

He glared at her. "And what is that?"

"It seems I'm not the only one who lied," she explained. "But at least I had a reason for mine. I can't think of one reason why you'd lie."

His face darkened, and his eyes narrowed. "Mrs. Holt, I do not lie."

Her brows arched. "Really? Then how do you explain your letter?"

"My letter?" Then, as if he suddenly remembered

what he'd written to her, his tone changed. "My letter."

"That's right, Mr. Gardiner. Your letter. You lied. Would you like to read it again to refresh your memory?"

"No," he answered. "I don't need to read it. I remember exactly what I said."

"You said you had a small farm and you were far from wealthy—"

"I apologize for my choice of words—"

"Your choice of words? Is that what you call it? Where I come from, it's called a bald-faced lie." Audra couldn't keep the anger out of her voice. "You had the nerve to accuse me of lying when you did exactly the same thing."

"I did have my reasons."

"Oh, and what reasons are those?"

"They don't matter now."

"They matter to me," Audra insisted. "Reasons for people's actions do make a difference."

He let out a huff of frustration. "This is not the time or the place to discuss it," he said matter-of-factly. "I'm hungry. I'm tired, and I want to get back to Stonehaven before it's too dark to see where I'm going." He flicked the reins and turned his attention back to driving the wagon.

Audra fumed. She couldn't remember ever being so angry. How dare he dismiss her as if her concerns weren't important? She was about to point out that he was being a complete boor when

Thomas let out a wail and began wriggling in her arms.

Thomas's cries grew louder as they neared the house. He was likely hungry and she only hoped there was somewhere private she could feed him before his screams deafened everyone within miles.

Before the wagon rolled to a stop in front of the house, the door opened and a plump, gray-haired woman hurried outside. She stopped at the side of the wagon and her eyes widened when she saw the squirming bundle in Audra's arms. "Oh…"

Neall climbed down and heaved Audra's trunk out of the wagon bed and took it up to the porch. When he came back a few seconds later, he held out his arms. "I'll take him while you climb down."

Audra hesitated. He was still angry. That much was obvious, and she wasn't sure he'd even know how to hold an infant.

"I do understand your reluctance," he muttered sharply, "but I can handle a horse that hasn't been saddlebroke. I think I can handle a baby."

"He squirms."

Neall held out his arms, his lips twitching. "I promise I won't break him."

Audra wasn't so sure, but she allowed Neall to take Thomas. Gently, he settled the baby's bottom in the crook of one of his arms, wrapped the other arm around his back and held him against his chest. The cries miraculously stopped and Thomas's head rested against Neall's shoulder for a moment before he wriggled until he could look up at Neall's face. He blew a bubble. then he reached up, grabbed Neall's nose and gave him a gummy grin.

Audra held her breath until she saw Neall's lips spread in a smile and a laugh escape. Maybe she'd misjudged him, Audra thought, at least as far as dealing with children went. Taking her eyes off Neall and Thomas, she quickly got down and came around the wagon to take the baby back.

As soon as Thomas was safely back in her arms, Neall climbed back into the wagon, flicked the reins and drove off, heading toward a large barn near a group of smaller buildings a few hundred yards away.

Audra watched him go, disappointment gnawing at her. She'd hoped that during the trip from Austin, they'd be able to talk about the situation. Instead, it seemed to have made matters worse.

The woman came to stand beside Audra. "Welcome to Stonehaven, Mrs. Gardiner," she said with a smile.

Audra heard a faint Scottish accent in her voice. "Oh, no," Audra began. "I'm not Neall's wife. I'm Audra Holt. We were supposed to get married, but we didn't."

One of the few things Neall had mentioned on the way to the ranch was that he'd forgotten to let the pastor know he wouldn't need his services after all.

"Heavens, there I go again letting my tongue loose," the woman said, shaking her head. "I'm Mrs. Davey, the housekeeper. I thought—"

"It's quite all right, Mrs. Davey," Audra assured her. "It was an honest mistake."

"First off, even though Neall won't consider calling me by my forename though he's a grown man now, you should call me Morag."

"Thank you, and I'm Audra."

Morag made a face at Thomas, who stopped crying long enough to give her a toothless smile. She held out her hand, and Thomas wrapped his hand around one of her fingers. She grinned. "Neall didn't tell me you had a bairn," she said. "It's been a long time since there's been a wee one in the house. It'll be good to hear the sound of a bairn's laughter again."

Audra couldn't help smiling. "This is Thomas," she said. "He's a little cranky right now because he's hungry."

Morag jerked her head in Neall's direction. "Is that why his knickers are in a knot?"

"No. It's a long story, I'm afraid," Audra replied. "We've had a…misunderstanding."

Thomas let out a screech.

"Well, now," Morag said, "let's get the bairn taken care of first. I'll put on a pot of tea and find you something to eat because I'm guessing you must be hungry, and then you and me'll sit down and you can tell me all about it. Come on, now."

Wrapping an arm around Audra's shoulders,

Morag led her and a very unhappy Thomas up the steps and into the house.

Audra paused inside the door, taking in the high ceilings and the gleaming wood floors. She quickly followed Morag up a wide staircase to a landing with six doors leading off it.

"Here you are," Morag said, opening one of the doors and ushering Audra inside. "Since you haven't said your vows yet, you can use this room. I'll get someone to bring your trunk up. Meanwhile, you have some privacy here to feed Thomas. When you're finished, come downstairs. Supper will be ready in an hour or so, but I've got a piece of cherry pie that should hold you over until then."

Before Audra had a chance to thank her for her kindness, Morag was gone. Knowing there was at least one friendly face in this strange house made her feel a little less worried about how she would get through the next two weeks with Neall.

She noticed a large overstuffed armchair in the corner of the room. She quickly sat down and prepared herself to feed Thomas.

As he nursed, she gazed around the room. A four-poster bed covered with a pale blue quilt filled one wall. A heavy bureau and wardrobe took up another. But it was the large window overlooking what seemed like miles and miles of land that drew her attention.

Cattle roamed freely on grassy fields that stretched as far as the eye could see. A few trees dotted the fields, and if she squinted, she thought she saw something sparkling in the distance. A river perhaps? She couldn't be sure, but maybe one day, she'd have the chance to find out.

His stomach full, Thomas dozed off in her arms a few minutes later. Carefully, she got up and laid him on the bed, then took two pillows and placed one on each side of him so he couldn't roll off and get hurt.

Leaving the door open so she could hear him if he woke, she left the room and made her way back downstairs. She couldn't resist peeking into the rooms as she passed on her way to the kitchen. The furnishings were solid and heavy, which suited a man's home, she supposed. The rooms were tastefully decorated and could have easily been found in one of the fancy houses back in Lincolnville.

The kitchen itself was bigger than Birdie's whole house, and well-stocked. Audra enjoyed cooking and she hoped she'd get the chance to try the huge cast-iron stove at least once before she had to leave.

Morag looked up from the pot she was stirring on the stove as Audra entered. "Ah, there you are," she said, resting the wooden spoon on top of the pot and crossing to a long counter stretching the entire length of the kitchen.

Two bone china cups, saucers and matching plates holding pieces of cherry pie were already set at one end of a wooden table that would seat at least eight people.

"Come and sit down." Morag dropped into one of the chairs with a huffing sound and patted the table beside her. Then she picked up the teapot and poured two cups of tea.

Audra crossed and took the seat. "This is very kind of you."

Morag waved away Audra's thanks. "Ach, 'tis nothing. I'm happy to have another female to talk to. Now eat your pie and tell me why you didn't marry Neall when you came all this way to do just that."

Audra was hesitant as she began to recount everything that had happened, up to and including Neall's withdrawal of his marriage proposal.

"I'm sure it's not as bad as it looks right this minute," Morag said when Audra was finished.

"I'd hoped we could at least talk about it, but as you saw, he stormed off."

Morag patted Audra's hand. "Don't you worry," she said. "I've known that boy almost since he was born, and he's a good man. Whenever he has a problem, he goes off into the barn and works until he's solved it. I'm sure once he thinks it through, he'll figure out something that'll work for both of you."

Audra gave Morag a faint smile. She hoped with all her heart that the housekeeper was right.

CHAPTER 4

Neall stabbed the pitchfork into the pile of hay and scooped up a forkful, then tossed it into Apollo's stall and closed the gate.

He couldn't decide if he was more disappointed or angry. Not that it made much difference to what he was going to do about the situation he'd found himself in, but it did make it harder to think straight when he couldn't decide how he really felt about being deceived. He'd been looking forward to getting married, to getting to know Audra and raising a family with her. He'd had high hopes for their life together, and suddenly, one tiny, red-faced infant had changed everything.

It wasn't the baby's fault, though. He'd had nothing to do with the lie, and he had no control over what his mother did.

Neall felt a smile tug at his lips. Strangely, when the baby had grinned at him, Neall's heart had done a strange little blip. And when the baby had gazed up at him and blown a bubble, he'd found himself mesmerized by the tiny rosebud lips and the huge blue eyes. Neall didn't understand his reaction to the baby, but he was in no mood to analyze it.

Audra's lie weighed heavily on him. Could he believe she'd really felt she had no choice but to deceive him and hope she could convince him to go through with the marriage once she arrived? Or had she had some other ulterior motive for her deceit that he wasn't aware of yet?

Maybe her plan was just to land herself a rich husband, and she'd hoped he'd be taken in by a child.

But she hadn't known he was rich, a voice in his head reminded him. She'd thought she was coming West to marry a man with a small farm who was barely making ends meet.

And she'd accused him of lying, too. She was right, and guilt speared him that he hadn't quite told the truth in his letter. He was usually honest, sometimes too much so, and he'd been a little ashamed of stretching the truth in his letter. He'd justified it to himself, telling himself it was the only way to find a woman who didn't care about his money. And, he'd told himself, in the end, what he'd written in his letter —and he still didn't really think of it as a lie—would improve her life.

She hadn't seen it that way, and she'd been furious. He didn't understand why she'd be annoyed at learning she'd be wealthy and live a life of luxury.

She'd reacted as if she'd rather be poor, working night and day to eke a living out of a small parcel of land.

It made no sense at all.

Her lie, on the other hand…

A child, even though he was a beautiful baby, changed everything.

There was no way to know what had really happened, but deep in his gut, he sensed there was more to Audra's story than what she'd told him.

The question was, what was he going to do now?

One thing was certain. He had to go inside. Night had fallen while he'd been out in the barn and he'd likely missed supper. He couldn't hide forever.

Now that he'd calmed down somewhat, he needed to think. He'd give it some time. He'd let her settle in, get used to the house—and him. Then he would talk to her, listen to her explanation again with an open mind, and maybe he could figure out what to do.

Audra wandered through the rooms on the main floor of the house, pausing now and then to look at framed photographs on the tables and the mantel above a large stone fireplace in what Morag called the sitting room.

His floor-to-ceiling shelves were lined with thick leather-bound volumes as well as smaller books with covers showing landscapes, children, and gold-embossed letters.

She scanned the books, even though she couldn't read the titles, and chose one, running her fingers over the letters on the cover. She smiled, a nostalgic homesickness washing over her. Birdie had loved to read, and had often read to her when they were younger. Birdie always said a book could let her travel anywhere in the world and take any adventure she wanted to without ever leaving home.

Audra was so envious of those who could read. She'd tried, so why wasn't she able to make sense out of the lines? She'd gone to school, but she'd heard so often that she was dimwitted that she'd given up any hope of ever learning.

She didn't belong in a house like this. She'd expected to live on a small farm, not an … estate. And certainly not with a man like Neall—the way he looked and spoke, the house, all the books. He seemed far too…refined. Educated. Proper.

And far too handsome. So why would a man who had everything to offer a woman write for a mail-order bride? Why were no women in town willing to marry him? What kind of man was he that he couldn't court and marry a woman the way most men did?

Before she had a chance to think about it further, the sound of heavy footsteps reached her ears and a deep voice startled her. "Mrs. Holt?"

She spun around. Neall was standing in the doorway, a frown etched on his forehead. Her heartbeat tripled. Maybe she wasn't allowed in this room. Maybe…

His pointed gaze landed on the book clutched to her chest. Her face flamed. She'd forgotten she even had the book in her hands. "Oh…I'm sorry…I was just looking—"

"You're welcome to borrow any of the books in here," he said.

"Thank you." Not that there would be any point borrowing a book unless it had pictures. Oh, if only she could read … She'd never seen so many books in one place. She laughed inwardly. Maybe it was a good thing she couldn't read. She'd likely not live long enough to read all the books here, and choosing which ones to read would be almost impossible.

Guilt filled her. "Lies by omission are still lies," he'd said. She agreed.

He'd already rejected her. What more could he do to her if she told him the truth? Yet she couldn't bring herself to admit her failings.

She passed the book to him.

He took it and smiled.

It was only the second time Audra had seen him without a frown on his face, the first being when he'd smiled at Thomas. The transformation made him even more handsome than he'd been originally. His dark eyes twinkled and she noticed a tiny dimple near the corner of his mouth.

"You've chosen one of my favorite books —Frankenstein."

"I've never heard of this book," she said.

"The title is a little misleading," he said, opening the book and flipping through a few pages. "It's the story of a scientist who creates a monster."

She frowned. "I don't think I'd like that story."

"Yet it was written by a woman."

"She must be an unusual woman to write about monsters."

"You should read it one day and you can decide for yourself."

Did that mean he'd changed his mind and wanted her to stay? She wanted to know, but she was afraid to ask, so she kept her question to herself. "I may do that, but I prefer stories with animals or people… nice people. Like *Little Women* or *The Five Little Peppers*. Stories where the characters have adventures."

"Is that why you came all this way? You wanted an adventure, too?" he asked, handing the book back to her.

Audra considered his question for a moment. "I suppose that was part of it," she replied. "I came because I had no future in Lincolnville. This was an opportunity for a better life."

"On a small farm?"

"What's wrong with farming?" She'd known many farmers back home—honest, hard-working men and women.

He shook his head. "Nothing. Nothing at all. It's not an easy life. It's hard to imagine that you felt farming would be an improvement."

"It would," she told him. "I believed I was marrying a farmer, and that even though it would be hard work, it would provide a better life for me, and most of all, for Thomas."

"I see." He moved to the window, his back to her.

"Are you comfortable in your room?" he asked a few seconds later, breaking the silence that had fallen.

"I am, thank you," she replied. "It's a lovely room, and the view is wonderful."

"Good."

Long moments passed. A clock chimed in another room, breaking the silence that had fallen. "It's eight o'clock," he said as he crossed to the shelves, scanned the titles and plucked a thick book out. He tucked it under his arm. "I have some work to do. Sleep well, Mrs. Holt."

Without another word, he turned away and walked out of the room.

Neall dismounted and looped Apollo's reins around the hitching post in front of The Blue Sapphire the next morning.

The bell jingled when he opened the door to the diner and stepped inside. The smell of frying bacon reached his nose, reminding him he hadn't eaten breakfast that morning. He'd wanted to avoid Audra, and when he'd heard Thomas giggle through the closed kitchen door when he'd come downstairs, he'd turned and left rather than face the baby's mother.

Miranda was folding napkins at one of the tables. She seemed surprised to see him. "Good morning, Neall," she said with a smile. "What brings you to town so early? I thought you'd be spending time with your bride."

"There is no bride," he muttered.

Miranda stopped her folding and looked up at him. "What? Didn't she arrive on the train?"

"She did."

"Then what—?"

He leaned closer and gripped the edges of the table. "The woman has a baby!"

"I beg your pardon?"

"She has a baby," he repeated.

"Oh, how wonderful—"

"*Wonderful?* It's not wonderful at all," he contradicted. "If you remember, she didn't bother to mention that detail in her letter, and then, when she did get here, she didn't bother to even try to make an excuse for the lie."

"What did she tell you?" Miranda asked.

"She said she hoped it wouldn't make a difference to me," Neall said.

"And it does."

"Of course it does."

"Why?" Miranda looked genuinely curious.

"Because..." Why did it make a difference, other than the fact she hadn't told him first? He tried to come up with some reason why it bothered him so much, but every explanation he came up with was easily counteracted with common sense. "I want my own children," he told Miranda finally.

She tilted her head slightly and gave him a questioning glance. "You can still have children of your own."

"Well…I suppose that's true…but what if I can't care for Thomas the way I care for my own?" Even as the words left his mouth, he recalled the warm feeling he'd had when Thomas had smiled up at him.

Miranda reached across the table and rested her hand on Neall's arm. "I can tell you from personal experience that if you let yourself, you can love someone else's children as much as your own. I know you. If you give that baby a chance, I'm sure you'll love him just as much as any other child you might have in the future."

"I forgot you became an instant mother when you came here."

She grinned. "I did, and I've never regretted it. I love those two girls just as much as if I'd given birth to them myself." Her smile faded. "Have you told Audra what you're worried about?"

Neall shook his head. "We haven't spoken much at all."

"Then you need to talk to her and tell her what you've told me. Do you like her?"

"She's pretty, so I like that, but I don't know her well enough to know if I like her."

Miranda got up and picked up the pile of napkins. "Do you want my advice?"

He hesitated. Did he want advice he might not want to hear? He nodded.

"Get to know her before you make a decision. You might be surprised. If it turns out you still feel the same once you've spent some time with her, then I'll help both of you to find a solution."

Neall put his hat on. "You're right. Even though I don't mind a gamble, I've never been one to make snap decisions. You're a smart woman, Miranda. John's a lucky man."

Miranda smiled. "Let me know how things work out."

"I will."

Neall walked out into the morning sunshine. Miranda was right. He'd taken a chance. And until the train came through again, she would be his guest.

If nothing else, he'd been raised to treat people with respect, especially if they were guests in his house.

He didn't have to like her—or trust her—to treat her with kindness.

CHAPTER 5

*A*udra stood in the kitchen the next morning watching Morag as she mixed batter in a pottery bowl. Thomas was asleep, and the house was quiet.

"I thank you for your offer," Morag said, "but I've been looking after this house for more than twenty years. I have my own ways of doing things. Besides, you have a little one to take care of and if you don't mind me saying so, you look as if you're falling asleep on your feet."

"I'm fine, really …"

Morag looked over her shoulder to the long counter that ran the length of the room. "Oh, there is something you can do," she said, jerking her head. "I've forgotten how much flour I need in this cake. Take a look on that recipe beside you and tell me, will you? I left it over there so it wouldn't get dirty."

Audra's gaze landed on the piece of paper Morag

was talking about. Heat filled her face. It was going to be much harder than she'd expected to keep her ignorance a secret when she was living in the same house with people who thought she was smart enough to read.

Turning away so that Morag couldn't see her embarrassment, she crossed to the counter and picked up the piece of paper. The black marks blurred in her vision. She did recognize a few letters, but none of them made any sense. "I…I'm sorry, I can't read the writing…" she muttered and then set the paper on the table beside the bowl.

Morag sent her a confused glance but said nothing. She wiped her hands on her apron and crossed to stand beside her. "There it is," she said, running her finger across the paper. "Two cups. You couldn't read it?"

"Uh…no…I couldn't tell if it was two cups or three," she blurted out. "I think you're right. I must still be tired and my eyes aren't focusing properly."

"Aye," Morag said. "Or my penmanship. It isn't what it used to be."

"What kind of cake are you making?" Audra forced the conversation away from reading and writing.

"Just a plain pound cake," Morag replied. "I'm going to make a jug of custard to go with it for dessert. Has Thomas ever had custard?"

Audra shook her head. Custard was a luxury she'd never been able to afford.

"I'm sure he'll be licking his lips then," Morag said.

"Are you sure there's nothing I can do to help?"

"Not a thing." Morag scooped up a cupful of flour and added it to the batter. "You just rest and get your strength back."

So she wasn't needed—or wanted. The hope that she could make a home for herself here died. Neall would soon realize Morag didn't want her help and then she'd be right back in the same situation she was in back in Lincolnville. She'd have to leave.

Right now, though, she was so tired she could barely keep her eyes open. She'd fed and changed Thomas after she'd gone to her room the night before, then she'd undressed and climbed into bed. Thomas had gone back to sleep beside her, but she'd been so aware of his tiny body that she couldn't relax enough to sleep in case she rolled over and crushed him.

Not that she could have slept anyway, she mused. Neall's face had filled her vision every time she'd closed her eyes and the deep timbre of his voice had echoed through her mind.

He was everything the men she'd known in Lincolnville weren't—refined, polite, gentlemanly. Well, except for the lie he'd told that had brought her to Sapphire Springs. He'd still never explained why he'd sent for a mail-order bride when there were unmarried ladies in town he could have married.

And likely would marry once he sent her away. Sadness weighed on her. She didn't want to leave. If only she could find a way to convince Neall she wasn't a liar without admitting she couldn't read…

"Go and rest." Morag's voice interrupted her wayward thoughts.

"I am tired," Audra agreed. "I didn't sleep well last night."

"I can see that." Morag made a dismissive motion with her hands. "Now you get yourself up the stairs and I'll wake you when it's time for lunch."

Audra nodded obediently and turned to leave. Just then, the kitchen door opened and a man walked in. He was carrying something in his arms, and at first Audra couldn't tell what it was. Then she realized it was a baby's crib.

He was a large man, good-looking in a rough kind of way, and his smile revealed a tiny dimple beside his mouth that took away from the fierceness of the rest of his features.

He stood just inside the door and nodded. "Morning, Mrs. Davey."

Audra couldn't help noticing that the man addressed the housekeeper formally. Was it only her who called her by her given name?

"Don't you be tracking dirt in here, Tucker Gates," Morag scolded him.

"Yes, ma'am." Tucker looked down, adjusting his stance so his boots didn't leave the hooked rug under his feet.

"Is that it?" Morag asked.

"It is," he replied, setting the crib down on the floor. "I cleaned it up as best I could."

Morag inspected it thoroughly. "That's good. Thank you." Then, as if she just remembered Audra was there, took her hand and drew her toward Tucker. "Tucker, this is Audra Holt. Audra, this is Tucker Gates, the ranch foreman."

Audra held out her hand, and it was immediately buried in the man's huge hands. "It's nice to meet you, ma'am. It'll sure be nice to have a pretty lady here at Stonehaven to look at."

Audra felt her face warm. "Thank you, Mr. Gates."

"I'm just plain Tucker, ma'am," he said with a smile.

"Then you must call me Audra."

"Yes, ma'am."

"And what does that say about me?" Morag put in, planting her hands on her hips and peering at Tucker with a scowl. "Am I not the prettiest face you ever did see?"

Tucker's face flamed. "Oh…I didn't mean…uh… that is…"

Suddenly, Morag's face brightened and she laughed, her eyes practically disappearing into her wrinkles. "Ach, Tucker, you're always so easy to get a rise out of."

Tucker returned her smile, and before long, all three of them were chuckling.

Suddenly, Neall appeared in the doorway. His gaze settled on Tucker still holding Audra's hand.

Audra tugged it out of Tucker's grasp, guilt washing over her. Yet there was no reason for her to feel guilty. She'd done nothing wrong. So why did she feel as if she'd been caught in a compromising position? Heavens, Tucker had only been shaking her hand, nothing intimate at all.

Did Neall think there was something between them? Not that it would matter anyway, she thought. Neall had no interest in her and was going to send her away as soon as the next train came through.

"What's going on?" Neall asked. "What's that doing in here?"

"Tucker was just bringing your old crib in from the shed for Thomas," Morag told him.

"I see." Neall gave Tucker a pointed look. "Then unless the baby is going to sleep in the kitchen, I think Tucker should take it upstairs and then get back to work."

"Sure thing, boss." Tucker quickly heaved the crib back into his arms.

"I'll come with you—" Audra began, but Neall's voice cut her off.

"No need," he said to Audra before turning his attention to Tucker. "First room on the right at the top of the stairs," he said, stepping aside to let Tucker pass.

Audra slid a glance at Neall for a few moments. His closed expression gave no indication what was going on behind those dark eyes, but by the tone of his voice, she suspected he was angry. Why, she didn't know. Was it because he was under the impression Tucker was being too forward with her? Could he be jealous? Or was it nothing more than annoyance that the housekeeper had offered his crib to her without asking?

Whatever the cause, she refused to allow him to make her feel guilty. "If you'll both excuse me," she said abruptly, "I'm going to check on Thomas."

With her head held high, she stormed out of the room.

Neall watched Audra leave. She was angry, although he had no idea why since she'd been laughing when he walked in.

He'd never heard her laugh until then, and the sound had done something to him. It had seemed to slide through his veins, warming them until he'd wanted to join in.

Then he'd noticed Tucker's hand wrapped around Audra's, and the feeling had vanished. Anger had taken its place, and he'd snapped at his foreman. Why, he couldn't say.

Surely he didn't care if Audra and Tucker developed a relationship. That would solve the whole problem without any involvement from him. He wouldn't feel quite as guilty about going back on his word to marry her, and she'd have the husband she came for.

So why did seeing then standing so close together, laughing, her hand in Tucker's, make his chest squeeze until he couldn't draw in a deep breath?

Was it because for some reason he couldn't explain, he felt something for the woman who'd come to Texas to marry him? He shouldn't, because if he examined the facts rationally, which he always did, he'd know she was exactly the kind of woman he didn't want. He'd expected a woman he could trust, a woman he could spend his evenings with discussing books and music and current events, not one who seemed more at ease with a baby on her hip or knitting a…whatever it was he'd seen her knitting the night before when he'd passed by her open bedroom door on his way to his room.

Or was it purely lust for a woman who made his blood heat? A woman who tempted him to press his lips against hers, to feel her skin beneath his fingers?

Whatever the reason, he shouldn't have taken his frustration…and yes, he had to admit, his jealousy… out on Tucker. He'd never let his personal problems affect his relationship with his foreman or the ranch hands before.

He'd have to apologize to Audra, too, for whatever he'd said or done that had made her so angry.

Right now, though, he had something for Tucker to do at the far end of the ranch, a chore that would keep him busy enough that he wouldn't have the time or the energy to spend with Audra. And with any luck, by the time Tucker was finished, he'd know how he felt about Audra and whether he was willing to let her go.

Audra sat on the blanket under a willow tree in the yard behind the house. The sun blazed overhead, but in the dappled shade and with the faint summer breeze, it was perfect. Thomas lay beside her, gurgling as he grabbed at his toes and studied them. Since he'd discovered he could blow bubbles, he seemed to like the sensation on his lips when they burst. He'd smile his toothless smile and even laugh—a sound he'd just recently managed, but one that always made Audra laugh along with him.

She absently plucked a blade of grass from the lawn and stared out toward the horizon.

Tucker was out there somewhere, and she had no idea when he'd be back. The morning after he'd brought in the crib and she'd stormed out of the kitchen, she'd found out from Morag that Neall had sent him out to ride the fence lines. That was three days ago.

She couldn't help wondering if Neall had deliberately sent Tucker out to keep him away from her. Had he sensed Tucker's interest in her?

There was only one reason she could think of why Neall would care if Tucker spent time with her—jealousy. But why would Neall be jealous? He didn't want to marry her. He'd told her as much, so why would her relationship with Tucker—if a relationship ever developed—matter to him?

Tucker seemed like a nice man, and if she wasn't going to marry Neall, there was no reason she couldn't find another husband. And if Tucker was interested…

She was still pondering the situation when a shadow crossed her path. She looked up, squinting into the bright afternoon sunshine. Even in shadow, she recognized the breadth of Neall's shoulders, the way he stood, his knees locked, his thumbs hooked into the waistband of his pants.

"May I?" he asked, gesturing toward the empty space on the blanket.

She nodded.

With a grace that belied his size, he lowered himself to the blanket, taking a seat beside her and taking his hat off to let it dangle from one bent knee.

Locks of his dark hair tumbled down his forehead, and Audra had a sudden urge to reach out and brush them back. Instead, she tucked her hand into the pocket of her skirt.

For a short time, the only sound was that of a crow cawing somewhere in the trees. Finally, she heard him clear his throat. "I want to apologize for the way I spoke the other day. I should have apologized long before now, but I've been busy."

"I understand." She turned her head to face him. "Thank you."

"Would you like to see the rest of the ranch?" he asked.

She was surprised by the invitation, but immediately smiled and nodded. She hadn't been away from the house since she arrived. "I'd love to. When?"

"Now." He bounded to his feet. "I'll get a wagon."

"I'll have to dress Thomas—"

"I've asked Mrs. Davey to watch him, if that's all right with you."

She was hesitant to expect Neall's housekeeper to look after her child. After all, that wasn't her job and Audra already knew she was creating more work for the woman just by them being here. "Well…"

"I can assure you he'll be safe with her."

She smiled softly as Thomas let out a squeal of delight when he managed to wrap his fingers around one of his toes. "I'm sure he will."

For the rest of the afternoon, Audra listened as Neall told her about the ranch's history and described his plans for its future while he drove the wagon and showed her the pastures, the river, the closest line shack and the storage buildings dotted across the property.

She knew nothing about ranching and even though her questions sounded basic even to her own ears, he didn't seem to mind. In fact, he seemed pleased that she was interested.

For a few moments, he'd stopped the wagon on a

rise. As far as she could see, hundreds of cows…no, he'd explained ranchers didn't call them cows, they were cattle…grazed on the summer grass. "This is all yours?"

He nodded.

"What happens to them in the winter?" she asked. "If there's snow, they won't have anything to eat."

"We don't have as many head in the winter," he told her. "We split the herd and take some to market in the fall. It can get cold, but snow is very rare. They manage outside, and we make sure they have enough to eat so they won't starve."

"I hate to think of them being cold and hungry," she commented as they continued on.

He drew the wagon to a stop in front of a wooden crate-like structure nearby. "Then you'll really dislike this part of ranching. This is what we use to brand the cattle. We used to rope them and hold them down, but this is much easier and safer. I can't show you how it works right now, but next time we're branding, I'll let you know, if you're interested."

She couldn't help the shudder that engulfed her . "No thanks! That seems so …cruel."

"Unfortunately, it's necessary. Cattle look alike, so without branding, there would be no way to tell which ones belong to me."

Audra nodded in understanding. "I…thank you for this afternoon, but I should get back to Thomas," she said.

"Of course." He shifted in his seat and faced her. "I'm glad you came."

"I am too," she said softly. She'd seen the passion in Neall's eyes when he spoke about his ranch, and she understood. She was falling in love with the ranch, too. Or was it something else?

They rode in silence until they reached the house. Neall stopped the wagon and set the brake, then climbed down and came around to help Audra down. His hands spanned her waist, and for a moment, she felt herself falling into his arms, but he quickly steadied her and released her as if he'd touched one of the branding irons he'd told her about.

"Thank you again for this afternoon. I enjoyed it, and I learned a lot," she said.

He nodded and watched her turn away. She'd almost reached the porch when he called out. "I enjoyed the company, too. Would you have supper with me tonight?"

Since her first night at the ranch, he'd avoided eating his meals with her. Was he changing his mind about marrying her? Or was she reading too much into nothing more than an invitation to have supper? He'd told her he couldn't marry her because he couldn't trust her, but maybe this was a new beginning. A chance for her to give Thomas a good life. And if she was being completely honest, a chance for her to build a new life for herself with a man she was starting to care for.

She hesitated a moment too long.

"I understand if you'd rather not—"

"Oh, no," she replied quickly, sending him a bright smile. "I'd like that very much." She felt her cheeks grow warm, so before he noticed, she spun around and hurried into the house.

CHAPTER 6

*A*udra stood at the bottom of the stairs and pinched her cheeks to give them some color. She couldn't remember ever being so nervous. Her stomach fluttered like it held a thousand humming-birds and her heart skittered in her chest as she stepped into the sitting room.

Neall was standing near the fireplace, his back to her. He turned when she entered, and his eyes widened slightly. A slow smile creased his face. "You look lovely tonight."

Audra had taken pains with her appearance, and she was pleased her efforts had worked. She'd put on a peacock-blue cotton dress with pale turquoise embroidered flowers that she knew gave her skin a healthy glow and piled her hair on her head except for a few tendrils that framed her face.

She returned his smile, tempted to laugh. She needn't have bothered pinching her cheeks. His compliment had heated them more than enough. "Thank you," she murmured.

"Supper's ready," he said, cupping her elbow and leading her to a chair at the table in the dining room. He pulled the chair out and waited until she was seated before he took his seat across from her.

She glanced at the clock. It was a few minutes past six o'clock. She'd heard it chime as she opened her bedroom door. "I'm sorry if I kept you waiting," she said.

"You didn't. We did say six o'clock, didn't we?"

She nodded. Just then, the door leading to the kitchen swung open and Morag entered, carrying a soup tureen. She carefully set it on the table and ladled potato soup into two bowls.

As she was leaving, she met Audra's gaze and winked. Audra blushed.

"So," Neall said as he picked up his spoon. "Tell me about yourself, your life back in Pennsylvania. You mentioned you don't have any family there?"

Audra paused before answering, deciding which facts to admit and which to leave out. "That's right. I was an only child. My parents were killed in a carriage accident when I was eight years old and I was sent to live with my father's elderly aunt."

"I'm sorry…"

"It was a long time ago." She picked up her spoon and took a sip of the soup. It was delicious. She made a mental note to ask Morag how to make it before she left. "When I was sixteen, I met Tom, my husband,

and I married him the day after I turned seventeen. My aunt was happy to be rid of her 'burden' and I was happy to be out of a house where I wasn't wanted."

She paused, remembering how happy she'd been. "He was seven years older than me, and even though I didn't really love him when I married him, I did grow to love him. Not the way I'd always thought a woman should love her husband, but it was enough. He'd bought a small plot of land and we had such plans and dreams ..."

"What happened to him?"

Audra's throat tightened, and tears burned her eyes. She blinked them back. "We'd been married almost five years when I finally discovered I was going to have a baby. We were so excited that the months before Thomas was born seemed to take years." The memories rushed back, making it hard to go on. She took a few deep breaths, then continued. "Finally, the night came when I knew it was time. It was so dark, no moon, no stars to light the way. Tom rode into town to fetch the doctor. On the way back, his horse hit a gopher hole and threw him. The doctor said he was killed instantly."

She lowered her gaze and focused on the creamy soup in the bowl.

"I'm so sorry," he said. "That must have been difficult for you."

She nodded and looked at him, seeing the sympathy in his eyes. "It was. I couldn't believe Tom was gone and would never know his son. I couldn't look after the farm by myself so I sold it. My friend, Birdie, took us in. I had the money from the sale of the farm after the bank was paid back, but that only lasted a little while. I stayed with Birdie and I tried to find work, but there wasn't any. Then Birdie told me I had to leave because she was expecting another child and there wasn't room. When she saw your advertisement in the newspaper … well, you know the rest."

"I see," he said when she was finished. She met his gaze, saw the sympathy and understanding in his eyes and was glad she'd told him her story. She'd left out some key details, like the real reason there'd been no mention of Thomas in the letter, but at least he now knew why she'd had no choice but to become a mail-order bride.

The question was, even if he understood her motives, would he forgive her?

It had been four days since Neall had had supper with Audra, but she hadn't left his thoughts for more than a few minutes.

He couldn't remember ever enjoying an evening with a woman more than he had with her. They'd talked, and he'd discovered she had opinions about things most women didn't care about. She spoke intelligently and had met him point for point in a discussion about the role of women in society.

When he'd caught her trying to stifle a yawn, he'd suggested they say goodnight. He'd taken her hand in his, a sizzle of heat surging through him. He'd met her gaze, seen the desire in her hazel eyes.

Her lips had parted as if she was about to say something, but she didn't speak. Didn't move.

He'd wanted to kiss her. Wanted to find out if her lips were as soft as they looked. Wanted her body pressed against his.

He'd been about to close the gap between them when she tugged her hand out of his grasp. "I … better check on Thomas," she'd said. "Thank you for supper."

Then she'd turned and practically run out of the room, leaving him filled with… What was that feeling that seemed to fill every part of his body? Lust? Something more?

He'd been so busy since then that he'd barely caught sight of her.

Now, he stood on the porch, leaning against one of the posts, watching her as she played with Thomas on a blanket under one of the trees that dotted the yard. She was playing peek-a-boo with the baby, Thomas's giggles splitting the air every time Audra took her hands away from her face.

Neall smiled. Audra was laughing, too, and he couldn't help thinking about how pretty she was now that she was rested. Even though they were sitting in the shade, sunlight filtered through the leaves, making her hair gleam and casting her in a golden glow.

She leaned forward and scooped Thomas up in her arms, nuzzling his neck. Thomas giggled again.

She adored the child. That much was obvious. From what Mrs. Davey said, she spent almost every waking minute with the boy, and never complained when he woke during the night.

Neall wanted children to carry on his name. He'd known that for years now, but it had never been the right time to marry until recently. Now, watching Audra, he knew when he did marry, he wanted a woman who wanted children as much as he did, and who would be as devoted to them as Audra was to hers.

"Are you really thinking about sending her away on the next stage?" Mrs. Davey's voice snapped him out of his daydream.

"How can I marry her when I can't trust her?"

Mrs. Davey folded her arms across her ample stomach and stood silently beside him for a long moment. "Did it ever occur to you that she might have had a good reason for not telling you?"

"It did," he told her. "She told me why she lied."

"And?"

"I understand, but that doesn't make it right. She lied once. What's to stop her lying again?"

"People usually don't lie if they think they can be honest without being afraid of the consequences," Mrs. Davey said.

"She didn't give me a chance—"

"She didn't know you. She couldn't risk you

changing your mind when you read the letter. I'm sure she believed that once you met her in person, you'd accept her and her baby."

He didn't reply. He'd thought the same thing, and in the same situation where he felt he had no choice, he might have done the same thing. He didn't like knowing he could be capable of deceit, too, given the right circumstances.

But, a little voice inside his head reminded him, you are capable of deceit. You lied, too. You thought the woman—Audra—would be pleased to find out she was going to be a rich rancher's wife instead of the wife of a poor farmer, but it was still deceit.

"I've known you your whole life. You've always been fair and reasonable."

"This is different," he said.

"Maybe a little, but I've gotten to know her. You need to talk to her more, get to know her. You'll see soon enough what kind of woman she really is."

Mrs. Davey picked up her broom and began to sweep the porch, leaving Neall to think about what she'd said.

His gaze slid back to Audra, now holding Thomas in her arms, her head bowed. Maybe Mrs. Davey was right. Maybe he should give her a chance before he sent her away. If he didn't, he might regret it.

"…and me and the fish both went tumbling into the river." Audra couldn't help but chuckle at the story Tucker was telling her as they walked together while she picked wildflowers late the next afternoon. He really was funny. And kind. She was comfortable with him, as if he wouldn't judge her and find her lacking if she told him the truth about her stupidity. He was everything she'd hoped Neall would be.

But he wasn't Neall. Her heart didn't leap when she looked at him the way it did when she saw Neall. Her body didn't tingle when he smiled at her. And even though Tucker was good company and entertaining, he wasn't the man she wanted to spend time with.

Tucker was interested in her, she could see that much in his face whenever he looked at her. She could do worse, she reasoned. She might have to since it seemed Neall was going to send her away on the next train. But somehow she still hoped deep inside that Neall would change his mind before that time came.

She crouched to pick a purple flower.

"I'd better get back to work," Tucker said. "Here comes the boss. He's gonna be spittin' mad to find me here with you."

Audra straightened, frowning. "Why?"

"He's the one you came here to marry, isn't he?"

"Well…yes…but—"

His face flushed. "Audra," he sputtered. "I…well, that is…I like you a whole lot. You don't have to marry him if you don't want to. I'll marry you."

~

Audra didn't have time for Tucker's proposal to register in her brain before Neall was standing in front of them. "How's Fancy doing?" he asked, his face stern, his question directed to Tucker.

"She's been wandering all day," Tucker replied.

"Sounds like she's about ready then."

Tucker nodded. "I'll go check her again now." Turning to Audra, he tipped his hat and said, "I'll see you later."

"Who's Fancy?" Audra asked once Tucker was gone.

"She's one of the mares. She's about to deliver a foal, so we've been keeping a close eye on her."

"Oh…how exciting!"

"It is," Neall agreed. "It's something I make sure I deal with rather than leaving it to any of the hands."

Audra understood that.

"You're looking very pretty this morning," he said, changing the subject and giving her a bright smile that always made her heart skitter behind her ribs and her skin tingle.

That morning, she'd put on a yellow dress that always reminded her of sunshine and helped her mood, and she'd pinned her hair into a loose knot at the nape of her neck.

She met his gaze, her heartbeat suddenly racing. "Thank you," she replied quietly.

"I've been looking for you,"

That surprised her. "Why?"

"If Fancy delivers her foal today, I'm going over to Twin Pines Ranch tomorrow to buy two more mares," he said.

And? she wondered. What did that have to do with her? "Oh…"

"During our ride the other day, you seemed interested in the ranch and the way it's run, so I thought you might like to go with me—"

"I'd love to."

She was interested in all the day-to-day workings of the ranch, and the more she knew about how it was run, the more she could help him if he changed his mind and decided to marry her.

If there was a possibility he might one day care for her, she'd do everything she could to be the best ranch wife in the country.

But really, what chance was there? She wasn't the kind of woman he needed. She wasn't elegant and well-bred. She was a plain farm girl who couldn't even read or write.

He'd never look at her as a woman he could love and spend his life with. He already thought she was a liar. And once he found out she couldn't read or write, he'd know she was stupid, too.

Maybe she should accept Tucker's proposal. Then she wouldn't have to leave Sapphire Springs. She could marry Tucker and give Thomas a home and a father. Tucker was a decent man, a hard worker. She could do a lot worse.

Marrying Tucker would give Thomas a good life, and that was the most important thing in the world to her. If that meant marrying a man she didn't love, so be it. She'd traveled to Texas to marry a man she didn't love. What difference did it make which man it was?

The difference was that now, she was in love—with the wrong man.

Her breath hitched, the sudden realization filling her with both joy and sadness. Somehow, in the short time she'd been at Stonehaven, she'd fallen in love with Neall Gardiner.

CHAPTER 7

Something was going on between Tucker and Audra. Neall mulled it over as he rode out later that day to check on a calf that had been caught up in a mudhole but was now back with its mother.

And he didn't like it. Why it annoyed him, he couldn't say. He only knew that whenever he saw them together, the hairs on the back of his neck bristled and his gut tightened.

Audra and Tucker had looked awfully familiar earlier that afternoon, even though there was nothing inappropriate in the way they'd been standing close together, talking to each other.

She'd been smiling up at Tucker and it had been as if a stake was being plunged into Neall's chest. Then she'd laughed, the soft sound floating through the summer air to his ears. That she'd been laughing for another man bothered him more than he cared to admit.

Tucker wanted her. It seemed every time he turned around, Tucker was somewhere close to her.

Damn! He was jealous! There was no other explanation for the way his chest seemed to squeeze the breath out of him when he thought about Tucker and Audra together.

Audra had come west to marry *him*, not to be encouraging the attentions of another man.

But could he really blame her? She'd come to Sapphire Springs to get married. He'd told her she could stay until the next train, but then she'd have to leave. Why wouldn't she try to find another husband?

There was only one way to prevent her growing closer to Tucker and that was to marry her himself. Was he jealous because his feelings for her were growing? Or was he the kind of man who couldn't stand the thought of Tucker having Audra even if he didn't want her himself?

If he changed his mind and married her, he'd have to forgive her for her lie. He wouldn't enter into a lifelong commitment with resentment and distrust in his heart. But was he ready to change his mind? Was he ready to forgive her?

Audra paced her bedroom, restless and tired but unable to sleep. She'd gone to her room right after supper since Neall hadn't come back to the house.

She'd put Thomas to bed and tried to work on the

intricate pattern she was knitting, but couldn't concentrate, her mind wandering and random thoughts flitting through her mind. Tucker. Neall. The future. All so uncertain and worrisome.

Finally, she gave up and padded down the stairs to the kitchen.

"Is that you, Neall?" Morag appeared in the doorway of her bedroom attached to the kitchen.

"Where is he?" Audra asked.

Morag crossed to the window and looked outside. "In the barn. One of the horses is having her foal."

"Fancy," Audra murmured. "He told me about her earlier, but why is he out there? Can't Tucker or one of the hands—?"

"Neall won't let anybody else take care of the mares when they're foaling," Morag said. "He'll stay out there as long as it takes to make sure himself that the mother and the bairn are well."

Audra's heart swelled. He was rich and educated and all the things she wasn't, but he wasn't above spending a night in a barn taking care of one of his animals. Her respect for him grew even more.

"Is the coffee still hot?" she asked.

Morag nodded.

Audra crossed to the shelf and took down a mug. "Do you think he'd mind if I took him some?"

Morag grinned. "I think that's a fine idea."

A few minutes later, Audra opened the barn door and stepped inside. Scents of leather, manure and horse blended together, filling her nose. Light flickered from one of the stalls near the back and she carefully picked her way toward it.

She paused outside the stall and peeked in. Fancy was lying on a bed of straw, her breathing heavy, her chestnut coat shining with perspiration. Neall stood in the corner, watching every movement. Fatigue lined his face, a dark shadow of stubble covering his jaw. Still, he was the most handsome man she'd ever seen.

He looked up as she approached, his eyes widening in surprise. "Audra! What are you doing out here?"

She held up the mug. "I thought you might need coffee."

"You're right," he said, carefully picking his way around the horse so he didn't disturb her. Their fingers touched when he took the mug from her hand, sending a wave of heat sizzling up her arm. Her breath hitched in her throat.

"How is she doing?" Audra asked, stepping into the stall.

"So far she's fine. It shouldn't be long now."

"Do you mind if I stay?" she asked.

He gave her a slight smile. "I could use the company."

Averting her gaze from what was happening as much as possible, Audra crossed the stall and lowered herself to the straw near Fancy's head.

"It's best if you don't touch her," Neall said. "They like to be left alone."

Audra nodded. "Can I talk to her?"

"I suppose that wouldn't hurt."

Turning back toward the horse, she spoke softly. "It's all right, Fancy. It'll be over soon."

While Neall paced, drinking his coffee, Audra stayed by Fancy's head, doing her best to comfort her, her soft voice filling the stall with words of encouragement and sympathy. As the minutes ticked by, Neall's expression shifted, concern lining his features. "Looks like she's going to need some help," he said. "She might get ornery, so you'd better move away."

Audra nodded an acknowledgement that she'd heard Neall's warning, but kept up her soft chatter as she moved farther away from the mare but still doing her best to keep Fancy calm.

Audra watched as Neall worked to deliver the foal, his face etched with worry. "It's a colt," Neall announced proudly when, after what seemed like hours, the foal was delivered safely.

Within a few minutes, Fancy got to her feet, her movements so sudden that Audra had to scramble out of the way, landing on her backside near the wall.

Fancy waited, watching as her foal struggled to get up on spindly legs that didn't look strong enough to support him. He toppled over a few times before finally managing to stay on his feet.

Fancy moved to stand beside her colt and licked his face.

Tears sprang into Audra's eyes. She was completely entranced. She'd never witnessed an animal's birth, but she understood a mother's love…

"Are you crying?" Neall asked, his voice filled with concern. "Did Fancy hurt you?"

"No," Audra replied, quickly brushing her tears away. "It's just so ..." She shook her head, unable to find the words to describe the emotions surging through her.

"I know," Neall said, closing the gap between them. "I feel the same way every time."

Audra gave him a watery smile. "You look exhausted," she said. "Now you can get some sleep."

"I need to stay for a while longer to make sure they're both out of the woods. You should go inside, though." He took out his pocket watch. "It's getting late."

"I'd like to stay."

His eyes searched hers, and he sank to the straw beside her. "I'm too tired to be much company, but I'd like you to stay."

His arm grazed hers but he didn't move away, just leaned back against the wall of the stall, crossed his ankles and folded his arms across his chest.

Audra was mesmerized watching Fancy and her colt get to know each other, but the shadowy light and the silence soon lulled her into that place between wakefulness and sleep. She felt Neall shift. His arm draped around her shoulder and drew her toward him until her head rested on his chest.

She was warm. Protected. Secure.

She thought she felt his lips on her forehead as she slipped into sleep, and she smiled.

Audra leaned on the split-rail fence the next afternoon watching the horses prancing in the corral at Twin Pines Ranch while Neall negotiated the sale of the two mares with Hubert Schaab, a giant of a man with a bulbous red nose and sprigs of grayish hair.

She'd been tempted to invent a headache to avoid going with Neall that morning, but she was worried he'd know she was lying. She couldn't afford even a tiny fib if she ever expected him to trust her again.

She'd been mortified the night before when he'd gently woken her after a couple hours and told her Fancy and her colt were fine and they could safely go back to the house. She'd quickly tugged herself out of his arms and raced into the house and upstairs to her room. She was still awake when Thomas began fussing just after dawn.

Neall hadn't mentioned anything when she'd joined him at the wagon after breakfast, and as they rode to Twin Pines Ranch, she'd begun to relax and enjoy the ride.

The sun beat down, but she hardly noticed, her attention caught in the antics of the horses. She'd never ridden a horse. Growing up, her family had no need for a horse, and once she married Tom, he'd rented an ox from one of the neighboring farmers for plowing. She'd often thought how freeing it would feel to have the wind in her hair as she rode.

"They're going to grow into fine ranch horses," Neall's voice interrupted her memories.

She turned her head to look up at him and her heart swelled. "Which horses did you buy?"

He pointed to two horses—one brown and white, and one solid chestnut. "It's not final yet," he replied. "Hubert has written out a bill of sale but I haven't signed it yet. I wouldn't mind getting a second pair of eyes on it before I sign it. Care to take a look and see if you notice anything I should be concerned about?"

Her pulse raced and her breath caught in her lungs as he handed her a piece of paper. Swallowing thickly, she focused on the paper, her eyes narrowing as she concentrated on the handwriting. She recognized a letter or two, but nothing else. She held the paper out for Neall to take it back. "It's really not my place…"

"I thought you'd be interested—"

"Oh, I am!" Heavens, how could she explain she'd love to talk to him about the terms of the sale, but she had no idea what was written on the paper? She chuckled, the sound brittle to her ears. "I don't know anything about buying horses," she said, trying to make light of her ignorance. "Now if you were buying a new hat…or a new stove…I'd definitely have an opinion."

He smiled softly. "Fair enough."

"If you've read it carefully, I'm sure it's fine."

He nodded. "I'll just go and finalize it then, and

once I hitch them to the back of the wagon, we'll head back to Stonehaven."

She watched him walk away, her heart sinking. She loved him. She knew that. But loving him wouldn't be enough.

Neall slid a glance at Audra sitting beside him in the wagon. As soon as they'd left Twin Pines, he'd sensed her mood change. For a few minutes while they'd talked about the bill of sale of the colts, she'd seemed anxious. Her body had tensed; her smiles had been forced.

Yet as soon as he'd helped her into the wagon and they'd set off back toward Stonehaven, he'd noticed her relax and the stiffness in her body had softened. The question was, why? What was it about buying the horses that had caused her to suddenly appear distressed?

She obviously wasn't afraid of horses. If she was, she wouldn't have gotten so close to Fancy the night before, and she wouldn't have been so eager to come with him. And she certainly wouldn't have spent time alone, watching them, while he was inside speaking with Hubert.

Besides, she'd seemed fine until he asked her to look at the bill of sale. Unless…unless she had trouble seeing properly. Did she have bad eyesight? Did she wear spectacles and was trying to hide that from him?

Did she think he was so shallow that he wouldn't accept a woman who couldn't see well without them?

He couldn't think of any other reason why her brows would have knitted together as she tried to read the bill. If her eyesight was an issue, surely Mrs. Davey would have seen it. He made a mental note to ask her when they got back to the ranch.

"You seemed to enjoy the horses," he said. Her response might give him a clue why she'd seemed on edge at Twin Pines when he'd asked her to look at the contract…unless she lied again. Still, now that he half-expected it, he was sure he'd be able to tell.

She looked over at him, her eyes bright, her smile wide. "I did. They're beautiful."

"Maybe once they're saddlebroke, we could go riding." The words slipped out before he even realized it.

Her gaze darted to his. "What—?"

"I mean…" What had he done? For a few seconds, he'd forgotten she'd be leaving in a few days. It would take weeks before the mares were ready to ride. Audra would be back in Pennsylvania by then. "Nothing."

He flicked the reins, urging the horses to move faster. The sooner he got back to the ranch and away from Audra, the better. His thoughts jumbled when he was around her, his good sense disappearing like a puff of smoke in a windstorm.

Audra nodded and he noticed her shift on the seat enough that her back was turned slightly away from him. She sat straight, as if she had a length of iron up her back, her hands clasped tightly in her lap. Her eyes were glued to the landscape and she stayed quiet for the rest of the way back to the ranch.

Once they got back to the house, he helped her out of the wagon, his hands on her waist. He couldn't bring himself to release her. "Audra——" he began.

She looked up at him, her face flushed. "Thank you for today."

"I'm glad you came," he said. And he was. More and more, whenever they were together, a sense of calm and comfort filled him, while at the same time, his senses were heightened and his desire for her rose to a new level. It was all very confusing.

"I should get back to Thomas…" Her voice was breathy, heightening his senses.

"Oh…yes…of course…" He drew his hands away from her waist. With a tiny smile, she took a step back. Was she as reluctant to leave as he was to let her go?

"I'll see you later," she murmured, gazing up at him for several long moments before she climbed the porch stairs and opened the door to the house.

He couldn't let her leave. Not yet. She was about to close the door behind her when he called out. "Audra."

She looked over her shoulder toward him, her hand still resting on the doorknob. "Yes?"

In long strides, he bounded up the stairs and into the house, kicking the door shut behind him and stopping mere inches from her. He took her hand and drew her toward him. "Oh, hell…I feel like a schoolboy…"

Tiny creases appeared in her forehead and her head tilted slightly. "What is it? What's wrong?"

He'd never been so nervous around a woman. What was wrong with him? Before he could stop himself, he blurted out the words he'd been practicing all the way home. "I…I want to kiss you."

He heard her breath hitch and saw her cheeks flush. She said nothing at first, but her lips quirked in a smile that took his breath away. When she finally spoke, her voice was little more than a whisper. "What's stopping you?"

Audra's heartbeat thundered against her ribs and her breath caught in her throat. A slow tingling sensation flowed through her, weakening her knees as he wrapped his arms around her waist, his fingers splaying across her back.

Her soft curves met his hard muscles and his mouth slanted over hers in a kiss that was both tender and demanding.

She was lost.

She'd loved Tom, but even though she'd liked his kisses, she'd never reacted to his touch the way she reacted to Neall's.

She let herself relax against him, wrapping her

arms around his neck, threading her fingers through his coarse hair.

He wanted her. And she wanted him. It was a heady sensation.

For a mere second, he drew away and their eyes met. Her lips parted and he kissed her again, his tongue plunging inside, tangling with hers.

Sensations she'd never experienced before swept through her, both exciting and frightening her. She sensed deep in her core that she should have had these same feelings for Tom, and for a moment, guilt threatened.

Then Neall's lips left hers and rained a trail of kisses along her jawline to her neck where her pulse was raging.

The faint sound of hoofbeats blended with the rampant beating of her heart. "Neall," she whispered, the word a half-moan, half-sigh.

Neall drew away and she looked up at him. For a few seconds, she could do nothing but try to steady her heartbeat while he stared at her with such an intense expression in his dark brown eyes that she forgot to breathe.

The hoofbeats grew louder and then stopped seconds before Tucker threw open the door and stepped inside the house.

CHAPTER 8

$\mathcal{T}$ucker's brows arching when he saw Neall and Audra together at the bottom of the stairs, but he didn't comment, just took off his hat and raked his fingers through his hair.

Audra's gaze flitted between the two men for a split second before she spun around and raced up the stairs to her room.

Neall glared at Tucker. "What?"

Tucker paused for a moment before asking, "Everything okay, boss?"

Everything was far from okay, but for once, he wasn't about to share his thoughts with his foreman. "What is it, Tucker?"

"I wanted to talk to you, but if it's a bad time…"

"It's fine," Neall replied. "What do you need to talk to me about?"

"The cabin out by Spruce Creek."

Neall frowned. The three-room cabin had been vacant for years. "What about it?"

"I was wondering if you'd be okay with me moving out there rather than staying in the bunkhouse with the rest of the boys," Tucker said.

"Why would you want to do that?"

"Well…Audra and me—"

Audra? Neall's heart thumped. "What about you and Audra?"

"Well…" Tucker's hands squeezed the brim of his hat. "She told me you and her weren't getting married and she was supposed to leave on the next train."

Neall nodded, a lump forming in his throat.

"She told me she doesn't want to go back East," Tucker went on, "so I told her I'd marry her."

"Do you love her?"

"I don't know her well enough to love her yet, but I figure it's time I got me a wife, and I think in time I will. She is a pretty little thing and I figure she'll warm my bed well enough. She's nice, too, and a good mother to that baby of hers so I'm guessing she'd be a good mother to any children we'd have together."

Neall's fists clenched and his stomach twisted at the thought of Tucker and Audra … together in the most carnal way. Audra carrying Tucker's child…. Neall's lungs refused to take in air. "What…did she say?"

"She hasn't said anything yet, but I figured I'd see if we could live in the cabin. It needs some work to fix it up for a woman, but I could do that when I'm finished my regular work for the day."

Neall didn't answer. He needed to think. Not about the cabin. He didn't care about the cabin. He needed to think about who would be living in the cabin. Audra and Tucker. Together.

"What do you say?" Tucker asked.

Neal wanted to tell Tucker he was fired and to get off his land before nightfall. Instead, he sucked in a calming breath. "I'll think about it."

Tucker nodded. "I'd best get back to work now," he said, then planted his hat back on his head and left.

Neall heard the door close behind him as he stepped into his study and slumped into the chair behind his desk.

Audra lay on her bed, her heartbeat still thundering in her chest, her fingers resting on her kiss-swollen lips. Something incredible had happened to her, something she'd never be able to forget.

In all her years of marriage, she'd never felt the way she had in Neall's arms. She'd loved Tom, expected to spend her life with him, and was quite content. But until now, she'd never realized she was missing anything. Now, the way her body had reacted...craved...his touch, she wanted...more. More of something she could never have.

Tears burned her eyes. She loved Neall with all

her heart, but even if he was growing to care for her enough to marry her, she couldn't spend the rest of her life hiding the fact she was dimwitted. He was an educated man, a businessman. What kind of wife could she be when she couldn't even read a recipe or a bill of sale?

She could pretend for a while. She knew that. Over the years, she'd become an expert at hiding her ignorance, but when he found out… No, she couldn't live the rest of her life with him, loving him and knowing he resented her for yet another lie. A lie by omission, but a lie nonetheless.

Tucker had proposed to her. She could have a good life with him. Her deep-rooted sense of decency warred with her need to protect and provide for Thomas. Could she really marry Tucker even though she knew it wasn't fair to him, that he deserved a woman who would love him the way she loved Neall?

She looked over at Thomas asleep beside her. Her heart overflowed with love for her sweet and innocent child. Brushing her thumb across his baby-soft skin, she let her tears fall.

"Good morning. Where's Mrs. Davey?" Neall asked the next morning when he went back to the house and found Audra chopping apples at the counter in the kitchen. He'd avoided her the evening before, using ranch work as an excuse to skip supper and stay out until he knew she'd retired.

He'd stayed in the barn long after dark, using lantern-light to catch up on chores while the men went back to the bunkhouse and the windows of the house darkened. He'd missed seeing Audra at the supper table, missed the conversations he'd quickly grown used to during their evening meal, missed teaching her the finer points of backgammon in the evening.

It was just as well, he told himself. If she accepted Tucker's proposal, he'd have to get used to spending his evenings alone again. A deep sadness filled him at the thought.

"She's out in the garden."

Neall noticed she wouldn't look at him, keeping her gaze concentrated on her task. Was she annoyed with him? The way she'd run off when Tucker walked in…as if she'd been caught in a compromising situation. Which they would have been if the door had opened a few seconds earlier.

Was she feeling guilty that she'd allowed him to kiss her? That she'd kissed him back?

His glance slid to the apple in her hand. "Are you going to throw that peel over your shoulder and find out the initial of the man you'll marry?" It was a silly superstition he'd heard, but now, he couldn't help hoping she would toss the peel, and that it would land in the shape of an "N" on the floor.

She shook her head. "It has to be in one piece,

and I've already torn it in two." To prove her point, she put the knife down and lifted two strips of peel.

"Maybe next time," he uttered.

"Is there something I can do for you?" she asked, picking up the knife and going back to peeling the apples, still avoiding his gaze.

"I only wanted to let her know I'm going into town this morning and I'm not sure when I'll be back."

"I'll tell her."

"Thank you." He turned and opened the door, paused, then closed it again. He spun around and crossed the kitchen to the table. "I'd like you to go with me," he said. "I do have some business to take care of, but if you need anything for yourself or Thomas at the mercantile…"

She finally looked up, her cheeks flushed. Was she embarrassed about their kiss?

"I need to finish chopping these."

"Mrs. Davey can do the rest."

"Thomas—"

"Mrs. Davey loves the boy, and I'm sure she'd be happy to keep an eye on him."

"I—"

"Are you going to avoid me forever because I kissed you?"

Her face reddened even more. "Not, not at all…"

"Then come with me."

"Well…all right."

"Good. I'll let Mrs. Davey know, and I'll wait for you outside."

As he crossed the yard toward the kitchen garden a minute or two later, his thoughts wandered back to the kiss they'd shared the day before.

He shouldn't have kissed her. It had made matters so much worse now that he knew there was a possibility that she'd be marrying Tucker.

The kiss had excited him in ways he'd never expected. He'd known lust before, and usually a visit to the brothel in town took care of it. He'd never known lust arising from feelings of…love.

He loved her. Loved her enough to put her lie behind them. Loved her with every cell in his body, every breath that he took. Even Thomas had wound his way into his heart. Whenever he saw the baby, his tiny arms reached out so that Neall could take him. Audra had shown Neall how to do strawberry kisses on Thomas's cheek, making the baby giggle uncontrollably, which always set Neall off too. Yes, he thought, Miranda had been right when she'd told him he could love Audra's son like his own.

He knew Audra well enough by now to know that she would fulfill her obligation to him and marry him if he asked her to. But was it too late? He wouldn't force her to marry him if she'd fallen in love with Tucker.

His chest tightened. There was only one way to find out. He'd have to ask.

Audra stood in front of the mercantile later that morning, one small package in her arms. Before he left her at the store to take care of his own business, Neall had told the storekeeper to put her purchases on his account. She couldn't bring herself to take more of his charity than she absolutely had to but she did buy a yard of cotton flannel to sew a few diapers for Thomas, since the ones she'd brought with her were so thin they were practically useless.

Sweeping a glance down the street, she searched for a sign of Neall, but couldn't see him anywhere. The wagon was sitting in front of the mercantile, so she put her package in the wagon bed and set off.

She hadn't had a chance to really see the town of Sapphire Springs the day she arrived, and since she could keep one eye on the wagon for Neall's return, she decided to take a stroll down the street.

As she passed the millinery shop, she paused to admire one of the hats in the window. Oh, how she'd love to wear something frivolous and delicate, she thought, instead of the one homespun bonnet she owned. Still, she couldn't see herself ever buying something so impractical even if she had all the money in the world.

Moving on, her thoughts drifted back to Neall. Where was he? What was he doing now? He'd barely mentioned their kiss that morning, which had surprised her. She'd expected him to…what? Apologize? To profess his love for her? She shouldn't care. She knew that. Heavens, if she was thinking at all about marrying Tucker, she shouldn't be thinking about Neall at all. She shouldn't be reminiscing about the way his mouth had slanted over hers, about how strong his arms had been when they'd wrapped around her, how hard his body was when he'd pressed her against him.

And she certainly should not have been dreaming about him the night before.

Forcing thoughts of Neall out of her mind, she slowly made her way to the edge of town until the only other buildings in front of her were the Wells Fargo office and the livery stable. The stagecoach sat in front, four horses already harnessed and ready to leave.

Such a horrible journey to get to Sapphire Springs, she recalled. Her fear of the unknown, the discomfort, the filth and barely edible food…she couldn't bear to think of having to make that same trip again to go back East.

She caught her reflection in the window of a narrow building, and behind her reflection, she saw a man stepping out of the Wells Fargo office across the street.

She spun around, her heart slamming into her ribs. Neall was standing on the boardwalk outside the office, and as she looked on, he slipped something into the pocket of his shirt.

Something that looked suspiciously like the blue ticket that had brought her to Sapphire Springs.

Her throat squeezed shut and she found it hard to draw a breath.

He'd bought a train ticket to send her away.

CHAPTER 9

*A*udra was waiting in the wagon when Neall strolled toward it a short time later. It took every ounce of inner strength not to show how miserable she was, and she forced a smile to her lips when he greeted her.

"Are you finished shopping already?" he asked, looking into the back of the wagon. "You hardly bought anything."

"I didn't need much, just some fabric."

"For new dresses? Not that you don't look pretty in the dresses you have already, but they're awfully thick to wear in summer here."

She shook her head. "Diapers for Thomas. I don't need dresses." She wouldn't need them back in Pennsylvania. "Are we going back to the ranch now?"

Neall took out his pocket watch and flipped it open. "It's not very late," he said. "Why don't we have lunch at the diner? I could use a piece of the best cherry pie in Texas and you can meet Miranda and John."

She wanted nothing more than to be alone and try to figure out what she was going to do if she went back East, but she'd barely eaten anything at breakfast and her stomach was beginning to object. "Fine."

A few minutes later, Neall ushered Audra into The Blue Sapphire. The mouth-watering aromas of roasting beef and coffee met her nose and she sniffed appreciatively.

A young woman with a mass of auburn curls looked through an opening in the wall at the rear of the diner and grinned. She turned away and spoke to someone, then hurried out to greet them. "Neall! How nice to see you," she said as she wiped her hands on the white apron around her waist. Behind her, a tall man followed. When they both stopped in front of Audra and Neall, the man draped his arm around the woman's shoulder and hugged her to his side.

"And this must be Audra," she said, a wide smile on her lips.

Neall smiled back and made the introductions. "Since it's because of you Audra is here, I thought you might like to meet each other."

"I was hoping Neall would bring you by for a visit," Miranda said to Audra.

Neall took off his hat. "Can we eat first? I'm starving."

"Then you'd better sit yourselves down." Tucking

her hand beneath Audra's elbow, Miranda led her to a table, leaving Neall to follow behind. John mumbled something about talking to Neall after lunch, then hurried back to the kitchen.

"The menu's on the board," Miranda said once they were seated at a small table near the window. "I'll leave you two for a minute to decide. Would you like coffee?"

Neall arched his brows in Audra's direction. She nodded. "Yes, please."

Miranda left and Neall focused on Audra. "You're awfully quiet," he said softly. "Is everything all right?"

"Fine." The lie slipped from Audra's lips.

"Good, because there's something I want to talk to you about—"

Here it comes, she thought, her stomach sinking. This is where he would tell her he didn't want her and he'd bought a train ticket back to Pennsylvania.

"Here we are." Miranda suddenly appeared at her side and set two cups of coffee onto the table. "I'll bring the sugar and cream right away. Have you decided what you want to eat?"

Neall took a quick look at the chalkboard on the wall. "I have. Audra?"

"Oh…" Audra followed his glance, squinting at the white lines. What was she going to do?

"Are you having trouble seeing that far?" he asked.

"No! Not at all," she protested. "It's…it's just so hard to decide…"

"Everything is good here," Neall put in.

"I can come back," Miranda offered.

"No…" That wouldn't help. It wouldn't matter how much time she had, she wouldn't be able to read the writing.

If only she'd thought quicker when Neall asked about her eyesight. That would have been the perfect excuse why she couldn't read the menu.

She studied the board for a few seconds and suddenly, she found a solution. Turning her attention to Neall, she grinned. "I'll have whatever you're having," she said.

Neall gave her a curious glance, but didn't say anything, just nodded. "In that case, two orders of chicken and dumplings."

After Miranda left, Neall unfolded his napkin. "I don't even know what your favorite food is."

"I'm not a picky eater," she told him. "Chicken and dumplings is one of my favorites."

"Mine, too."

"Does Morag make it for you?"

"No. It's the one thing she's never been able to make as well as Miranda does."

"I'll make it for you one day," Audra told him. As soon as the words left her lips, she realized what she'd said. She wouldn't be making chicken and dumplings, or anything else, for Neall.

"I'd like that."

Her throat tightened. Luckily, Miranda arrived with their meals just then, and for the next several minutes, they ate quietly other than occasional comments about the food.

Once the plates were cleared and Neall had finished the cherry pie he'd been looking forward to, Audra put her napkin on the table and took in a calming breath.

Neall hadn't lied when he'd said the food at The Blue Sapphire was delicious, and normally, she would have enjoyed every bite. This time, though, she'd had to force it past the lump in her throat. Now, even though she dreaded the words that would slam the door on her hopes, she realized she might as well hear them and get it over with. "What was it you wanted to talk to me about?"

"I…we'll talk about it later," he muttered, putting his fork on his plate and sliding it away from him.

"Why not now?"

"Later." Suddenly he stood up. "I need to talk to John for a minute before we leave. I'll ask Miranda to bring you more coffee if you want it."

"No, thank you."

She watched him walk away and disappear into the kitchen area. Moments later, Miranda hurried out. Wiping her hands on her apron, she crossed to the table and slid into the chair Neall had just vacated.

"I've been dying to meet you," Miranda said, resting her elbows on the table and leaning toward her. "How are you and Neall getting along? Are you getting married soon?"

Audra wasn't quite sure how to answer. She thought for a moment, deciding she might as well tell the truth. "We're not getting married at all. He doesn't trust me and doesn't want to marry me. I just saw him coming out of the Wells Fargo office, so I'm guessing he was there to buy a train ticket for me to go back to Pennsylvania."

"I'm so sorry," Miranda said, reaching over and squeezing Audra's hand. "He did tell me about your baby."

"I was wrong to keep it from him," Audra admitted.

"I'm so sorry. I really hoped you'd be able to work things out."

"I hoped so, too, but there's no time left. From what I understand, the train will be leaving from Austin in two days."

"Until you board that train, there's time. John and I had problems, too. It's not easy marrying someone you don't know. It takes work to build a relationship, a good marriage. I almost left, too."

Audra was surprised to hear that. From what Neall had said, Miranda and John were very much in love. "You did?"

Miranda nodded. "Both John and I had things… private things…we were dealing with. If we'd brought those troubles into the open and talked about them…"

"But you did eventually?"

"We did, but it took a while, and I was ready to

leave and go back East. I'm so glad I didn't, though. I won't say it's always been easy, but I've never been happier. If you don't want to give up, tell him how you feel. At least you'll know you did your best to make it work."

Audra thought about what Miranda had said while Neall paid the bill and they got into the wagon to go back to the ranch. Could she tell Neall the truth about her feelings—and her secret shame? Could she marry Tucker and see Neall every day, knowing she would never be his? Or should she leave, go back to Lincolnville and try to somehow build a life alone for herself and Thomas?

Neall drove away from town, trying to still the stampede of wild buffalo in his stomach. He couldn't remember ever being so nervous, and now, the woman sitting so quietly beside him in the wagon held his future—his life—in her hands.

He couldn't stand it one minute more. As soon as he found out what was on Audra's mind—and it was obvious to him that something was on her mind— he'd ask the question that had been nagging at him since Tucker's pronouncement the day before.

He tugged on the reins and waited until the wagon stopped and then shifted in his seat to face Audra.

Her face was tense, but even so, she was beautiful.

Her hands were clasped tightly in her lap, and she'd barely spoken a word since they'd left the diner.

"Audra," he said softly, prying one of her hands away from the other and burying it in his. "What's wrong?"

A slow flush crept into her cheeks. "Why…nothing… I'm fine…"

"No, you aren't, and I wish you'd tell me what's bothering you. You seemed fine… well, to be honest you seemed a little distracted this morning on the way to town," he said, a wry smile tugging at his lips, "but since I met you after you finished your shopping, you've barely said a word. Did something happen in town that you don't want to tell me about?"

"No," she replied. "Everyone I met was very kind."

He studied her for a few seconds. "And Miranda? What did you two talk about?"

She didn't answer immediately, and Neall couldn't help wondering if he'd been the subject of their conversation. "She told me about her and John," she said finally.

"That's all?"

Her voice softened. "She asked if we were getting along and when we were getting married. I told her we weren't."

What was that expression in her eyes? Sadness? Worry?

He looked away. He couldn't think straight when he looked at her. This was it—time to find out if she was going to marry Tucker, even though Neall's chest felt as if a dagger was embedded in his heart. "Tucker told me last night that he'd asked you to marry him."

Audra's face reddened and her mouth formed a perfect "O".

"Did he?" he pushed.

Audra nodded.

"And? Will you?"

She straightened in her seat, held her head high and met his gaze. "Does it matter to you?"

His throat tightened. She had no idea just how much it mattered to him. "It does," he replied, his voice cracking.

"Why? I came to Texas to marry you. You refused. Why does it matter to you what I do now?"

"It matters because…" *Because against my better judgment, I've fallen in love with you,* he wanted to say, but the words stuck in his throat. He couldn't bring himself to open his heart to her until he knew how she felt about Tucker. "Because you're living in my house—"

Her eyes darkened, and he realized his words had hurt and angered her. Why, he didn't know, but they'd triggered a response that shocked him.

"That may be," she snapped, "but only for two more days and then you'll be rid of me."

His chest constricted at the thought he'd never see her again. But would it be worse to have her living with Tucker, knowing she loved him, slept in his arms…? Her sharp tone interrupted his thoughts.

"The ticket to Lincolnville I saw you buy this afternoon—"

"What?" His voice seemed to fill their surroundings. "What ticket?"

"I saw you coming out of the Wells Fargo office with a ticket in your hand."

"A ticket," he repeated, his voice barely more than a whisper.

"Yes. A ticket."

He reached into his pocket and drew out the piece of blue paper she must have seen him with earlier.

"You mean this ticket?" he asked.

He held the ticket out for a moment so that Audra could see the words on it, then dropped it into her lap. "Read it."

The ticket fluttered in the soft breeze, and she picked it up before it got carried away. She stared at it for what seemed like minutes but was only a few seconds before she looked away. "Did you read the destination?" he ground out. "San Antonio."

Her gaze shifted back to the ticket. "What—?"

"Mrs. Davey is going to visit her cousin in San Antonio next week. She asked me to pick up her ticket."

"Oh…" The sound was little more than a sigh.

"You thought the ticket was for you to leave?"

"Why wouldn't I? It's what you told me the day I arrived, that I could stay at the ranch until the next train came through and then you'd send me back."

He had said that, but he hadn't loved her then. Now…losing her, whether she went back East or married Tucker, left a hole in his heart that would never heal.

"I shouldn't have said that. I…"

He plucked the ticket out of her hand and slid it back into his pocket. "So, are you going to marry Tucker?"

"I don't know." She glared at him for several long moments, then climbed out of the wagon and began to walk toward the house.

"What are you doing?" he called out.

"Walking the rest of the way," she answered, not bothering to turn around when he spoke.

"Why?"

"It helps me to think."

"I don't want to leave you out here—"

She stopped and turned to face him. She looked up at him, and for a second or two, he thought she might change her mind and get back in the wagon. Then she shook her head and stepped to the side of the rutted trail. "Please. Just go."

Their gazes met and held until finally, Neall flicked the reins and the horses moved slowly past her and he left the woman he loved behind.

He loved her! And because he loved her unconditionally, he forgave her for what she'd done. He did understand her motive for her lie—protecting her child. In fact, knowing what lengths she'd go to in order to secure her child's future made him love her even more. It meant that no matter what happened in the future, she'd do whatever she had to do to keep her children safe.

He only hoped those children she had would also be his.

CHAPTER 10

The sun had dipped beneath the horizon by the time Audra reached the ranch house, and still she was no closer to making her decision.

Marrying Tucker wouldn't be fair to him, but it would secure a future for her and Thomas. If she was honest about her feelings when she spoke to him later, and he still wanted her, would that ease the guilt that seemed to weigh her down whenever she thought about spending her life with him?

She wanted to spend that life with Neall, but that wasn't to be. So wouldn't marrying Tucker be her best option?

Audra trudged up the stairs and opened the door. A wail assaulted her ears.

Hurrying up the stairs, she rushed into the bedroom and found Neall trying to comfort Thomas. Thomas was squirming in his arms, his lips pursed, his face mottled red.

"I'm trying, but he doesn't like me much right now."

Audra smiled softly at the screaming infant and held out her arms to take him. Thomas quieted instantly when she held him close to her chest and whispered softly to him.

Neall looked on. "I can calm a skittish horse that's twice my size, but apparently a tiny bundle like Thomas is beyond me."

"Babies are like animals. They sense fear," she said with a chuckle.

"I'll leave you to it then."

She didn't speak, just watched him walk away and close the door behind him.

"What should I do, Thomas?" she asked the baby. "If I don't marry Tucker, I'll have to go back to Lincolnville. If I do marry him, I'd be the best wife I could, but I'd never be able to love him. But living so close to Neall, loving him and knowing he doesn't love me back…"

Her heart felt as if it were slowly being torn apart.

Thomas couldn't answer her, couldn't give her any advice. All he could do was give her a toothless grin, gurgle, purse his lips and blow a bubble, warming her heart.

A bittersweet smile tugged at her lips. "That's what I thought."

~

Neall placed the bookmark in the book in his lap and looked up as Mrs. Davey came into the sitting room later that evening. "Do you think Audra has trouble with her eyesight?" he asked.

The housekeeper set a cup of tea beside his chair and straightened. "I don't know," she replied. "Why do you ask?"

"I showed her the ticket I picked up for you and she peered at it as if she couldn't see the letters. Have you ever seen her wear eyeglasses?"

"No, but I do recall her saying she couldn't read the handwriting on a recipe," she said. "I was surprised. The penmanship was as plain as day."

"It was the same at the diner earlier today. She squinted at the menu on the chalkboard on the wall as if it was too far away to read."

Mrs. Davey straightened the crocheted doily on the back of the settee near the fireplace. "If that's the problem, why bother to hide it?"

"You tell me. You ladies and your pride. Could she be embarrassed about wearing eyeglasses? Is it possible she thought I wouldn't want to marry her if I knew?"

"It is," Mrs. Davey admitted. "There are some men who'll turn away from a woman because of it."

Neall took a sip of the tea. "Thank you, Mrs. Davey," he said absently.

"Audra!"

Neall's voice carried through the silence in the house and reached Audra as she passed the doorway to the sitting room on her way to the kitchen.

She paused, her nerves tingling, her heartbeat skittering. He didn't sound angry, but his voice was loud enough that she couldn't pretend she hadn't heard him.

On trembling legs, she took in a calming breath and went into the room.

Neall was sitting in an armchair reading one of the leather-covered books that lined the bookshelves, the planes and lines of his face shadowed by the lamp on the table beside him.

Her stomach tingled just as it did every time she saw him these days. She recognized the sensation, wishing things were different, wishing he loved her as much as she loved him.

She wanted to feel his lips on hers again, wanted to be wrapped in his arms once more, wanted to be so close to him that she could feel his heart beat against hers.

But there was no point wishing for something that could never be.

"Is Thomas asleep?" he asked.

"He is," she replied. "He was hungry and needed changed, that's all."

"I'll admit he scares me a little," he said. "I don't know anything about babies and I was afraid I'd break him. Since he's asleep, do you have time to keep me company?"

"I…suppose so…"

He opened the book. "Do you like poetry?"

"Some," she replied.

"My mother used to read to me when I was young," he said. "I enjoy being read to. Do you?"

"My friend, Birdie, used to read to me. Not poetry, though. Stories. I'd close my eyes and I could see the story in my mind, and let the words seep into my heart."

He began to read, his voice soft and hypnotic. The poem was about being wrong, about atoning for mistakes. When he was finished, he got up and moved to sit beside her on the settee.

He took her hand in his, his warmth flowing through her. Her nerve endings tingled, a sensation deep in her stomach that she recognized whenever he was near.

"We started off wrong and I'm afraid I might have misjudged you," he said. "Now I have an important question to ask you, but I want you to promise to tell me the truth."

He was so serious it frightened her. She nodded.

"Do you have trouble with your eyesight?" he asked.

He'd asked her the same question the day they'd gone to Twin Pines to buy the new horses. Why was he asking her again? "No," she replied.

"You don't wear eyeglasses?"

"No, I don't. I told you I have no trouble seeing the last time you asked."

He smiled, but it didn't reach his eyes, and his voice sounded…disappointed. "I mistakenly thought your eyesight might be the reason why you seem to avoid reading."

Her cheeks burned with shame and guilt. "I…I don't avoid reading…"

"The recipe. The bill of sale at Twin Pines Ranch. The menu at the diner. I assumed you couldn't read them without eyeglasses."

He opened the book and handed it to her. "You have such a lovely voice. Please read this to me then. It's one of my favorite poems." He leaned back and closed his eyes.

Audra stared at the printed words on the page. She couldn't think of one good reason why she couldn't read the poem to him.

A few seconds later, he opened his eyes and looked up at her. "You don't like that poem?"

"It's not that…"

"Then what is it? Why won't you read it to me?" His voice took on a suspicious tone. "Or were you lying to me again, telling me your eyesight is fine when it obviously isn't."

Anger, shame and sadness overwhelmed her. Still, she held her head high and slammed the book shut. "I did not lie. My eyesight is perfect."

"Then read the poem."

This was it! She'd have to tell him the truth. She'd

be leaving Neall's house in two days anyway so what did it matter now if she admitted how stupid she was? Her voice quivered when she spoke again. "I…can't."

"Why not?"

She lowered her head, not willing to see the derision in Neall's eyes. Humiliation overwhelmed her. "Because I can't read."

She got up, leaving the book on the settee where she'd been sitting and stood with her back to him, facing the bookshelves.

Silence filled the room and she'd begun to wonder if Neall had quietly left when she felt his hands curve around her shoulders and turn her to face him. "You can't read," he repeated finally with as much surprise in his voice as if she'd told him she wasn't really a woman.

"That's right." Her cheeks burned. She might as well tell him everything. "And I can't write either."

"Why didn't you tell me?"

She let out a bitter laugh. "Telling the man you hope to marry that you're stupid isn't something a woman does."

"Just because you can't read does not mean you are stupid!" His voice grew louder. "Did you go to school at all?"

She nodded. "I tried to learn, but the letters got mixed up. The teacher told my parents I was dimwitted and too stupid to learn anything, and that I'd be lucky to find a man who'd take me. Birdie tried to teach me to read, but I still couldn't learn. That's why, when she told me about your advertisement, I couldn't bring myself to tell you."

"The letter…" he murmured, as if he'd just remembered it. "Then…you didn't write the letter."

She shook her head. "Birdie wrote it for me."

"Did you tell her what to say?"

Audra searched her brain, trying to remember. "Not really," she said. "I thought she'd tell you everything. I don't know why she didn't tell you, and I couldn't write to ask her."

"I see," he said.

"So that day at the train station, you really believed I knew about Thomas."

"I did."

"And I thought you were lying. I didn't handle it well when I found out. I expected a lone woman."

"And I thought you wanted both of us," she said.

"It seems we were both wrong."

She pulled herself out of his grasp. "It doesn't matter now," she choked out, then ran out of the room.

It doesn't matter now.

Neall repeated Audra's words to himself over and over again as he sat alone in the sitting room. What did she mean? Was she going to marry Tucker?

He loved her. He was pretty sure he'd started falling in love with her the day she arrived, even though he'd fought it. He'd never stop loving her, and he couldn't let her marry Tucker without her knowing how much he loved her.

She was upstairs in her room with the baby. All he had to do was climb those stairs and tell her how he felt. It was a risk. He knew that. It could be too late. But he was willing to take the chance. The reward would be more than worth it if his gamble worked.

The knock at the bedroom door startled Audra. Wiping the tears from her cheeks, she opened the door, expecting to see Morag.

Instead, Neall stood in the hallway. He barged in and closed the door behind him.

"This is highly improper—" she began.

"I don't care," he said. "Before you go off and marry Tucker, there's something that needs to be said, and I'd rather Mrs. Davey didn't hear it."

Audra's heart thumped in her chest. "What is it?"

His gaze bored into hers. "I don't want you to leave," he said quietly.

"You don't?"

"Because…you came here to marry me, not Tucker. And…" His voice lowered to little more than a whisper. "I love you."

Hope flickered inside Audra's chest. Hope that dimmed when the reality took hold. "I came to Sapphire Springs expecting to marry a man with a small farm, a man who came from the same kind of background I did. I can't be the kind of wife you need. I'm not refined, or elegant, or educated. I can't even read a sentence."

"You're exactly the kind of wife I need—beautiful and kind and sweet. And a woman who takes my breath away and makes me want to wrap her in my arms and never let her go." His gaze raked over her. "And the woman I want to make love to all night long, and hope she'll be the mother of my children."

Audra flushed.

"But—"

"As for reading, your teacher didn't know how to teach you. That's all."

"She taught the other pupils. They learned."

"Everyone learns differently," he told her. "Your teacher didn't know how *you* learned. But if you want to learn to read, you can still learn."

Audra took a step closer. "I do want to learn, but the letters get mixed up."

"Then we'll find someone who can teach you how to unmix them." He took Audra's hands in his and drew her toward him until they were mere inches apart. "It doesn't matter to me if you can read or not, if you wear spectacles or not. None of it matters to me. What matters is that I love you, your heart, your spirit, all of you. And if you love me, too that's all that matters."

Audra's eyes stung with unshed tears and her throat tightened. "I do. I do love you."

He kissed her then, tenderly, with a promise of a future together. When he finally released her, she was breathless.

Then he got down on one knee. "I should have done this the day you arrived, and I hope it's not too late. Audra, will you be my wife and let me adopt Thomas so he's my son?"

Tears streamed down Audra's cheeks, but they were tears of happiness. She nodded. "I will."

A sound from the crib beside the bed drew her attention. Thomas blew a bubble, then grinned and let out a gurgle.

Audra laughed and looked up at the man she loved, the man she was going to spend her life with. "Thomas approves."

eall stood on the front porch of the house, looking out across the fields to the river.

Audra sat in the shade of a nearby tree reading *Alice's Adventures in Wonderland* to Thomas while Penny, their three-month-old daughter, played with her toes on a blanket beside her.

He was amazed at how quickly Audra had learned to read once he'd hired a tutor who was experienced in teaching adults to read. Now, she almost always had a book in her hands when she wasn't looking after the children or spending time with him.

These days, she corresponded regularly with her friend, Birdie. When she'd written to Birdie to ask why she hadn't mentioned Thomas in the letter, she'd admitted she'd just forgotten. She'd been so concerned about Audra's future that it had slipped her mind.

It didn't matter now. His life was finally perfect.

He crossed the yard toward Audra and his children, his heart filled with love. He'd never really believed he could find the kind of love his parents had had for each other. Now he knew he'd found just that, a love that would last until his final breath.

"Supper will be ready soon," he said when he stopped at the edge of the blanket.

Thomas wriggled off Audra's lap and launched himself into Neall's arms. Neall laughed, spinning Thomas in the air while the boy squealed in delight until Neall lowered him to the ground.

Thomas raced off toward the house while Audra got up and gathered Penny in her arms. Neall folded the blanket and draped it over one arm.

Then Neall wrapped his other arm around Audra's shoulder and kissed her softly. "Have I told you today how much I love you?"

"You have, but I never tire of hearing it. You know I love you more and more every day," she said with a smile, "and this has been a perfect day."

"It's not over yet," he said suggestively.

"I hope not."

Yes, he thought, as he gazed out over the ranch that would one day be his children's legacy. He was a lucky, lucky man.

KATHRYN, the third book in the Mail-Order Brides of Sapphire Springs series, is ready for you to read next.

Will tragedy heal the differences between a mail-order bride and her new husband, or tear them apart completely?

ABOUT THE AUTHOR

Margery Scott is the author of more than thirty sweet western historical novels, novellas and short stories. An avid reader, she didn't even consider writing her own books until her three boys were grown and she had an empty nest.

She now lives on a lake in Canada with her husband, and when she's not writing or traveling in search of the perfect setting for her next novel, you can usually find her wielding a pair of knitting needles or a pool cue.

Website: www.margeryscott.com
Email: margery@margeryscott.com
Newsletter: www.margeryscott.com/newsletter
VIP Facebook reader group: www.
facebook.com/groups/margeryscott